The
Expatriates

WILLIAM HAGGARD
The Expatriates

Hodder & Stoughton
LONDON SYDNEY AUCKLAND TORONTO

100786267

British Library Cataloguing in Publication Data
Haggard, William, *1907–*
  The expatriates.
  Rn: Richard Henry Michael Clayton   I. Title
  823′.914[F]

ISBN 0-340-49119-1

First published in Great Britain 1989

Published by Hodder and Stoughton,
a division of Hodder and Stoughton Ltd,
Mill Road, Dunton Green, Sevenoaks, Kent TN13 2YA.
Editorial Office: 47 Bedford Square, London WC1B 3DP.

Typeset by Hewer Text Composition Services, Edinburgh.
Printed in Great Britain by St Edmundsbury Press Ltd,
Bury St Edmunds, Suffolk.

CONTENTS

PART ONE

People

The raiding party was moving warily since it knew that a patrol must be quite near. Away to the east where the hills fell sharply, the frontier was guarded by an electrified fence; a road ran inside it and patrols went on wheels; but here in these hills – a couple of them were minor mountains – the frontier was ill-defined at best and tidy wiring out of the question. Patrols went on foot on a twisting track.

But what was possible to seal the Province had been thoroughly and expertly done. The theoretical frontier (only a single country recognised it) ran with the track through scrub and stunted trees, sometimes climbing, sometimes dropping as sharply. There was barbed wire everywhere. Where it had been practical it had been strung between trees to headheight and a little above, and where there weren't trees to carry it it had been laid on steel supports six feet high. Only six feet high but six yards in depth. There were re-entrants on the Greek side of the frontier which led to the broken track above them, and these had been given special treatment. To wire them effectively would have been next to impossible so instead they'd been thickly sown with AP mines. A notice at the re-entrant's mouth said that this had been done and it said it in Greek. Even so two men had already lost their legs. It was that sort of frontier, disputed and dangerous. Patrolled.

The raiding party lay hidden listening – listening for the patrol to pass them. It would take forty minutes to reach its terminal, perhaps twenty minutes rest, then another forty back to the same point. The raid had needed careful planning.

9

They had reached the re-entrant's mouth without difficulty, two thousand feet though little more than a scramble, but the last two hundred would mean serious climbing. For they didn't intend to risk the minefield: they meant to climb the re-entrant's left-hand wall, then work their way along the top to the track. The five Arabs had been taught to climb but the essential local Greek guide had not. Never mind. They would go up themselves, then pull him up on a rope.

So they lay silently till they heard the patrol. It was two hundred feet above them but quite close. It wasn't attempting to hide its presence, indeed could not have done so if it had wished. A dozen soldiers in boots and carrying arms made a good deal of noise on a stony path.

They waited till the patrol had passed, then the Arabs roped together deliberately. There was just enough moon to see hand- and footholds and the Arabs climbed with a cool professionalism. At the top they threw down a rope with a loop at its end. They had told the Greek how to sit in it safely, how to fend himself off from the rockface with his feet. He was evidently frightened but he'd been offered good money.

The night was still, the re-entrant windless till a malicious spirit puffed and the roped swayed. The Greek began to rotate as he swung, banging against the rockface helplessly. He started to scream and it sounded like a prayer.

A man on the rope said: "They'll hear that a mile away."

The leader said: "Then drop him."

He was more than halfway up but they cut the rope. The scream rose frenetically, then ended as though a knife had sliced it.

None of the five Arabs spoke a word.

At the top of the cliff it was easy going, sloping gently up to the path and the frontier. There was no wire here since there wasn't a need of it and they slipped across quickly into a thicket of stunted scrub. One of the five men asked:

10

"What now?"

"Not good," the leader said. "There's enough light to move but we don't know where to. Without that Greek we're as good as blind."

"We could follow the track till we see the mine's lights. They'll be a long way below us but we'll at least have a fix on it."

That was their target, the new mine in the Province. The old ones beyond the arbitrary border, in the part of the island which still spoke Greek, were exhausted or in increasing decay, but the new rulers of this unrecognised Province had struck it rich on a virgin vein. The pyrites weren't smelted locally but went away by sea to Israel where the trade was believed to make handsome profits.

Which was the reason these five men must cripple it. They were PLO who'd been admitted as refugees and had promised not to engage in politics. But their organisation had been much discredited, overtaken by others more ruthless and better financed. So they'd been ordered to do something spectacular, anything to restore a fading prestige.

The Arab said again: "We could follow the track. For a bit at least."

The leader shook his head at once. "And run into the returning patrol? We know how long it will take them to march but we don't know how long they will choose to rest. We could run into them head-on and have to shoot. That would be heard at the mine and alert it."

"Then what do we do?"

"We've all of us seen the sand-table model. From here there's a pretty steep fall for half a mile, then a very much gentler one for two miles to the sea."

"It's cultivated land with villages."

"That is something we know already."

"But without a guide – "

"If you wish to withdraw you have permission to do so."

11

It was an insult and intended to be so. The first man said stonily: "I shall now have to kill you".

"After we have completed the mission, please." The leader knew there would be no afterwards. None of them had a hope of returning; all of them were entirely aware of it.

They had carried rucksacks on their backs as they'd climbed and now they began to unpack them quietly. They held the barrels and stocks of Belgian machine pistols and these they put together expertly, loading them and slinging them with the ease which came from intensive practice. They put back their rucksacks but these weren't empty. They still held dynamite, wire and detonators.

It had been a scramble up the re-entrant behind them and it was another down to the coastal plain. Coming up they had been reasonably silent for they'd had time to pick their way and minimise noise; but time was now a remorseless enemy and they'd have to accept the risk of being heard. They went down fast, disturbing stones which rolled noisily, and once a loose scree slid for several yards. The noise was not in fact enormous, inaudible in the villages below them, but to the raiders it sounded like elephants panicking.

They had come down separately but at the bottom they re-formed into a tight knot. The leader looked at his watch and a compass. "We can't see the lights of the mine – that spur hides them." He waved an arm. "But we know where it lies, which is almost due west. We'll march. The sun will come up behind us soon." He looked at his watch again. "I give us ninety minutes dead. An hour to march four miles in the dark over country which we do not know, then half an hour to do the job. Any questions, please?"

There were no questions.

They began to march in Indian file. The moon had set but the sky was clear and there was just enough light to guide trained men. The fields weren't wired nor hedged nor ditched but every three hundred yards or so

12

they were cut by a considerable watercourse. It brought water from the underground lake and this water made the coastal plain prosperous. Once Greek and Turk had lived here together, if not in amity then at least without violence.

Not now.

They had had to make several detours from their route, where hamlets or a shepherd's hut had dictated that they couldn't march straight, and the leader began to look at his watch again.

"We're running it pretty fine."

"I know."

"We ought to be on a road by now, the one which leads to Ayios Theodor."

"God send we find it."

A friendly god sent and the five men changed formation instinctively. From Indian file they slipped to three and two, three men on the left of the road, two on the right, twenty yards gap between the two parties. Any infantryman would have recognised five others. He would also have noticed their considerable fire-power. Not that this was presently relevant since the last thing they wanted now was a firefight. That would come later when they sold their lives dearly.

Without the order given to do so they broke into the light infantryman's loping trot, making up the time they had lost in their detours. Soon they came to the broken gates of Ayios Theodor and stopped. None of them was breathing faster than normally.

They stopped because the silent village exuded an almost tangible menace. Other villages which they had skirted carefully had shown an occasional light or a dog had barked, but Ayios Theodor was entirely deserted. It was rather more than an average village, something less than an average market town, and once it had been wholly Greek. Its inhabitants had fled in a panic though in fact they had had no need to do so since unlike some villages down on the coast the Turkish troops here had behaved impeccably. Later civilian

Turks had come in but they hadn't stayed. The priest had laid a curse on Theodor with a half-forgotten rite of the Orthodox church. The Turks had cared nothing for Orthodox witchcraft but they had been peasants and were observant men. Curious things had begun to happen. Cattle began to die unexpectedly, children to sicken, wells to sour. There were noises in the night, apparitions. Within a month Ayios Theodor had been empty again.

The raiders had been told the story and as good Muslims they had put it aside, but as they trotted into the village purposefully one of them began to shiver. It was certainly an eerie place. The houses, some of them quite substantial, were barred and bolted but seemed undamaged, the main street which bisected the buildings was clean. But there wasn't a single light or a sign of life. A starveling cat ran across their path silently.

They came out on the other side and halted, unconsciously shaking their shoulders in unison. Nothing burdened them but the straps of their rucksacks but each of them felt he must shift some evil.

They had cleared the spur of the mountain which hid the mine and now they could see it below them, right-handed. It was in fact a miniature fortress, brightly lighted and heavily chain-wired. There were watch-towers at intervals in the formidable perimeter and in the centre, on a higher tower, a searchlight swept the surrounding ground. It had been cleared of all cover for eighty yards. In the centre the raw concrete buildings were huddled together like nervous cattle, the offices and two long barracks which housed the regular army Turkish guard. Beside them the mine's winding wheel rose starkly.

It was a considerable establishment but it was not the raiders' direct objective. It was hard to destroy a mine effectively, almost as hard as destroying an oil well, but the complex was four hundred yards from the sea and an aerial ropeway bore its spoil to the water, to the jetty where the Israeli ships loaded it. It was supported

14

by a series of pylons. If the raiders could blow two or three of these before men came from the camp and shot them down – if they could do this thing they'd have accomplished their mission. The mine would be useless for several weeks and stopping several weeks' profit to hated Israel was a well worthwhile target to men who detested her.

The leader looked at his watch yet again, timing the leisurely sweep of the searchlight. "Ten seconds exactly," he said, "Ten seconds. We'll have to move in in nine-second rushes. Drop as the beam comes near, then run again. Let's go."

There'd been a sense of evil in Ayios Theodor and all five raiders had felt it powerfully. Perhaps it had been powerful enough to blunt their normal sense of danger, for the mine, as they had later seen, was effectively a minor fortress, and like all good fortresses had posted pickets outside it. One of them had been in Theodor, in an attic in an empty house, and it had heard and seen the raiders moving. The officer had been a marksman and he'd had a sniper's rifle with an excellent nightsight. But he hadn't shot. There were five men here, correctly spread: he couldn't be certain of getting all of them. Instead he said to his sergeant:

"*Çavus*, get on the blower. Get me the commanding officer. Tell his duty dog to wake him at once."

There was a minute's delay before a strong voice said: "Yes?"

"Five men have just gone through the village. They were armed."

"Did you shoot?"

"I did not."

"You did well. Were they in uniform?"

"A sort of fatigues. I couldn't identify it."

"Were they carrying anything else but arms?"

"Not in their hands but they had outsized haversacks."

There was another short pause while the Major

15

thought. So it was what he was there to guard against, sabotage. "Thank you," he said, "I'll take all action necessary. That is the end of the message. Out."

He proceeded to redeem his word, giving his orders quickly and confidently. For this was a well-practised drill. The ropeway was outside the perimeter and it had been decided that it shouldn't be fenced. To do so would create a salient as pointless as that English General's. There weren't the men to patrol it regularly but nor was such patrolling necessary. Weapon pits had been dug on both sides and men could reach them in twenty-five seconds. The record in practice was twenty-two.

Moving in restricted rushes as the searchlight swung away on its long arc the raiders had made two hundred yards, forty from the hidden gunpits. They were moving now for the light was off them when unexpectedly it accelerated sharply. Its lazy wheel changed to a violent swing and caught them as they stood in its merciless glare.

Instantly fire raked them savagely. The men in the gunpits were professional soldiers and had held their fire for a certain target. Now they were firing at will and well.

Two raiders had dropped and the others followed them. The ground had been cleared of living cover but there was a fold in it which hadn't been flattened. The three men still alive fell behind it. The firing stopped.

Somebody said: "What now?" but he knew. His spittle was sour with the taste of failure.

For ten seconds there was total silence, then a mortar bomb burst twenty yards behind them. Another the same distance short.

The leader said: "Very good bracket."

"Yes."

"I'm not staying here to get blown to pieces. There's an outside chance we could take a few with us."

They rose together and charged the gunpits. One

of them was limping badly, all of them were firing furiously.

They never got near a single pit. It was magnificent and entirely insane. But they thought it a great deal better than capture alive.

Colonel Mehmet Eldem was woken at five o'clock in the morning. He knew that the call must be genuinely important for he was a man who liked a solid eight hours and had given very firm instructions that he shouldn't be disturbed over trifles. He picked up the telephone. "Yes?" he inquired.

"Major in command of the mine, sir."

"Speak."

"There's been an incident."

"What sort of incident?"

"An attack on the mine by what appeared to be terrorists."

"'Appeared' not 'appear'?"

"I have five dead men."

"Damage to the establishment?"

"None."

"Losses amongst your own men?"

"None again."

"I'll be out in an hour," the Colonel said. He corrected himself. "No, in sixty-five minutes." He had been to his Staff College where they'd taught him precision and in any case he had a tidy mind. He needed fifteen minutes to dress and shave and another fifteen to eat his breakfast; he wouldn't go out on an empty stomach. Then thirty-five minutes driving fast. "Understood?" he asked.

"It is understood."

At the guardhouse by the perimeter gates the guard turned out and saluted smartly. The officer detached himself and gave Mehmet Eldem another salute. This *Albey* was an important man.

"Good morning, sir."

"Good morning, Major."

17

"Will you come into the office, please?"

"Later. First I'd like to see the bodies. I suppose they really are all dead."

"The doctor says they are very dead."

"A pity," Mehmet Eldem said, for he would have relished one alive to interrogate. The raiders had done him a crude injustice in fearing the torture they practised themselves. For physical torture was out of date: nowadays there were techniques more reliable. Mehmet hadn't been trained in their use himself but he had a Captain who had taken a course in them.

Also a doctor who didn't ask questions.

The Colonel said: "I'll look at them first."

"Then come with me, sir."

They had been put in the punishment cell in a neat row. Mehmet Eldem asked a routine question though he knew very well what the answer would be. "Any identification?"

"None."

"Then who do you think they are and where from?"

The Major stroked his carefully shaven chin. "They look like Arabs to me," he said at last.

"Indeed? Pray tell me, then, what Arabs look like."

The Major told him in a sibilant monosyllable.

The Colonel was a little shocked, not at the obscenity but at a generalisation which he considered unjustified. This Major was an excellent soldier who would probably make Lieutenant-Colonel but Mehmet who'd seen the wide world outside Turkey considered him distinctly conventional. He said in gentle reproof but still reproof:

"I think that goes a little too far. Arabs are not my favourite people and the Ottoman empire was very well rid of them. Also they are indifferent soldiers or Israel wouldn't exist as a sovereign state. But it's unsoldierly to call them names."

The Major went to attention, said: "Sir!"

"It is forgotten. Let us return to business. There'll have to be a report, of course, something to show our civilian masters. All on cosy, reassuring paper. It will go to the

18

boss of this so-called Province and I shall also send a copy to HQ. In it I shall strongly commend you."

"That is very generous."

"No, fair. You carried out a duty successfully." Also, the Colonel thought, you were lucky. For any soldier that was very important. "Now let us return to the immediate problem which consists of five dead Arabs in a row. Any ideas for disposal?"

"Yes, sir. I thought we'd give them concrete boots, then take them out to sea and dump them."

The Major had been proud of this but surprisingly Mehmet Eldem said: "No. I won't have them treated like the substance you mentioned. After all they were a sort of soldier."

The Major was astonished and showed it. "Soldier?" he said. He was visibly shaken.

"I know what you're thinking and you're perfectly right. Soldiers are men in arms who serve a state. The PLO which these presumably come from is no state at all but a public nuisance. Technically these men are pirates. But they lost their lives in a cause they believed in. We happen to think that cause is mistaken and, worse, it is tearing three countries to pieces, but the fact remains these were men and brave ones. I won't have them dumped at sea like rubbish."

"Then what are you proposing, sir?"

"I shall send you five coffins. Not officers' coffins, that would take it too far, but the standard plain coffin for other ranks."

The Major was astonished again. "You're proposing to give them formal burial?"

"Certainly not, that's much too dangerous. We'd be lucky to do it without somebody noticing and the moment that happened the scandal would start to roll like a snowball."

Which is exactly, Mehmet Eldem was thinking, what I was sent here to prevent if I could. To suppress any awkward incident. To kill the news.

But the Major was saying: "Then how – ?"

19

The Colonel didn't answer directly. "When does the next ship sail for Israel?"

"On Thursday afternoon."

"Which gives plenty of time."

The Major stood silently, trying to make sense of it. Presently the penny dropped; so did the Major's mouth; he said:

"Israel won't like that at all."

"She can lump it." Mehmet Eldem admired the state of Israel for its realism and success in battle but he didn't feel the least affection. As for hatred that simply didn't arise. His country had an ancestral enemy and he kept all hatred strictly where it belonged.

He went back to his unobtrusive office and sent a coded report to his General in Turkey.

*   *   *

Mehmet Eldem had been disappointed when they hadn't made him a Brigadier but he could see the reasons they hadn't done so. Three years as a Military Attaché (with local rank as full Colonel, *Albey*) had given him some French and Italian, and since the longest part of this fruitful period had been spent in a country he liked, Great Britain, his English was fluent, correct and colloquial. These were assets in any currency known but they had distanced him from the command of men. He couldn't reasonably hope to make Brigadier.

The General who broke the news to him was by now much more than a simple General, in fact the most powerful man in the country, but he still liked to chair the quarterly meetings which decided senior army appointments. Mehmet was before one now and he had sensed that it was sympathetic; they weren't going to throw him out on the scrap heap. The General had begun to explain.

There was an island in the Mediterranean which had recently given a sackful of trouble. The Greeks had been getting above themselves, which they always did if

20

you didn't restrain them, treating the backward Turkish minority as though they had been helots. Which they were not. Finally it had got so bad that intervention had become inevitable. That intervention must be called successful. The Turks now had a Province of their own, and though only mainland Turkey recognised it it was efficiently run by a local boss. Moreover there had been no war, neither with Greece, which many Turks might have welcomed, nor, and this was much more important, with the then all-powerful United States. America had made disapproving noises but she'd taken no action to halt the invasion. She hadn't dared.

The General had paused. Was the Colonel following? Mehmet Eldem had said that he was.

Very well, then, that was the present position. It was stable enough militarily but in a bad way financially. The Province had not been the island's richest tract, depending largely on tourism and the expatriate settlers. The new mine was making a fresh contribution but tourism had dropped alarmingly. In the invasion some villas had been brutally looted by soldiers who had gone out of control. Quite senior heads had by now rolled accordingly and compensation had been paid out generously. So most of the settlers had quietly remained. But tourism still stayed obstinately down, the hotels were only half full at best. Hard professional publicity was doing its best but it wasn't a match for Greek malice and sabotage. There was nothing approaching an organised Resistance but men slipped over the border constantly, not yet terrorists but riffraff generally. They stole from the hotels and vandalised. Visitors felt endangered; they stayed away. At the moment the big hotels were near-bankrupt.

Something seemed required of Mehmet. "Very Greek," he said.

"I think so too." The General turned to another less senior. "You're in charge of the Intelligence side of it. The Colonel is entitled to know the worst."

So besides these Greeks there was still the PLO. The

21

South of the island had let them in, as much to show its contempt for the West as for any other motive visible, and their organisation had diminished in power. But they were still capable of some desperate last mischief, perhaps under pressure to risk some folly. And if rumour was right as it often was there was very much worse in the South than the PLO. They had started to let in men from Hezbollah.

The second general left it at that. He was a good soldier and had said his piece.

The chairman picked the story up smoothly. "So there's a need for an exceptional man, one who knows the world outside Turkey. I'm offering it to you as the best man available. Of course your staff will be very small since the last thing we want is to risk the impression that we're in some way intervening directly. That wouldn't suit our political book, nor that of the local boss whom they call the Man. We daren't incorporate the Province formally but without our backing it would surely collapse. So in effect you'd be my private ears and eyes."

"May I ask a question, sir?"

"Certainly."

"That mine you mentioned which helps the economy. How would I stand with regard to that?"

"How much do you know about that mine?"

Mehmet considered carefully before he spoke. "I know that a British company owns it. I know that it sends ore to Israel. I know that the pyrites it sends are in enormous oversupply throughout the world."

"Do you wish to know more?"

"Only what you may wish to tell me."

It was the General's turn to think and he did so; finally he said deliberately: "Guessing is not a court martial offence."

"But would I be responsible?"

The great man was not displeased but approving. Persistence was a virtue he admired. "I'm afraid your position would be somewhat anomalous but this sort of job is itself ill-defined. That mine is worked by Turkish sappers and guarded by a detachment from the troops which we keep there. With that you would not be directly concerned. The object of the job I'm offering is the suppression of anything – well any *scandal*. Anything which would attract the Press, locally or especially abroad . . . Unfair, you may think, but not all that so. You will have immediate and unquestioned access to the Man, and if you see something is not as it should be it will be part of your duty to tell him promptly. At a pinch you may come to me directly but that privilege is to be exercised sparingly. And I think you will find the terms acceptable. Your previously local rank of Colonel will be confirmed; your tenure will be several years and all of them will count for pension. I need not say a full Colonel's pension. Now what do you say?''

"May I think it over?''

The General frowned. "It's pretty urgent. How long do you want?''

"Can I have twenty minutes?''

This time the General laughed. "Very well.''

Mehmet returned in fifteen and said: "Thank you.''

The other members of the Board had left and the General waved Mehmet back to his chair. "Now you've accepted we can talk in more detail. I said there was no organised Resistance and it's essential that none be allowed to arise. A surprising number of Greeks stayed behind. Secondly these incursions from the South have got to stop. Individually they may be pinpricks but collectively, as I explained, they do damage. Last week these men switched from hotels to a house; they burgled one of the senior residents who went straight to the Man who in turn lost much face . . . What were the authorities doing?''

The General offered a long Latakia, politely lighting Mehmet's before his own. "And one other thing which affects us as soldiers. One of the people who lives in the Province is the daughter of the late Lady Withers. Her mother gave us vital help when we were forced into taking the action we did. We made her Colonel-in-Chief of one of our regiments and to the local Turks she's a heroine. If anything befell her daughter it would be more than a loss of face to myself; it would be an evident national shame and disgrace. Moreover I knew Lady Withers well."

"Does Miss Withers live in the Province permanently?"

"Not normally but at the moment she is. She kept the villa on when her mother died and usually uses it as a holiday home. If my sources are right and they usually are it is her custom not to arrive alone. But for the moment she is staying indefinitely, waiting for her lover to die. He's a terminal and a very brave man." The General rose. "Good fortune," he said.

But as Mehmet reached the door he fired a last shot. "From everything which I've heard from Europe you've done nothing to diminish our name but you're thirty-nine – no longer young. You're going to be in one place for several years, something which happens to very few soldiers. It's time you married and did your duty. Good day."

Mehmet had been in the Province a month, quietly absorbing the peculiar feel of it. He was comfortably settled in by now, finding a small flat with a view of the harbour and servants as befitted his rank. There was a man to look after his clothes and serve and a woman, who of course lived out, did the cleaning and was a tolerable cook. Both of them were local Turks.

His first call had naturally been on the Man and the two had got on well from the start. Mehmet had expected a certain resentment since his appointment had not been formally asked for but instead there had been an immediate welcome. The Man was an island-born Turk and looked it: his head was as round as a football and almost as big. But he came from one of the few well-off families and the knowledge that he was independent had given him a cool detachment

24

very rare in the island's frenetic politics. When it had been a single state he'd been a member of the central parliament and a Minister of some standing as well. When it had split he had gone to the North. He ran it pragmatically but with remarkable smoothness – something between a Mafia godfather and an old-fashioned Tammany Hall politician. Since no country but Turkey would accept his authority his constitutional position was nil. This troubled the Man in no way whatever. He got on with the business of running the Province. Mehmet had understood him at once. He wasn't a revengeful man; he wanted no further bloodshed of any kind; but Greeks were a fickle and volatile people, always dangerous if you didn't sit on them firmly. And in the South they were licking their wounds resentfully.

There you were.

He had given Mehmet a list of names, people with whom he should talk and whom he should hear. It was headed by the Maharajah, an exile but enormously rich, then the list had descended in smooth gradation through the local bigwigs like the President of the Club, through people of some means and standing such as Helen Withers and one or two others; and at the bottom the run-of-the-mill expatriates, retired soldiers and minor civil servants who were living on often inadequate pensions. Mehmet had worked through this list conscientiously and in the process had made a single friend. His name was James Wedder and, alas, he was dying.

On the morning after the raid on the mine Mehmet Eldem sent for his car and set out. He intended to pay a call on James Wedder whose opinion on local affairs he valued for he'd served in the State Department most of his life and had once been posted to this island before the split. He was a Scot by ancestry but by now was also an Old American, a good deal of established money behind him. There was a saying in the United States that the way to get on fast and surely was to go to Harvard and turn sharp Left. James Wedder had done precisely the opposite. He had gone to Yale and turned sharp

Right. He'd had an excellent academic record and the State Department had accepted him gladly. Now he'd returned to the island to die.

No, that wasn't quite right, it oversimplified, but it also increased respect for James Wedder who, when the last days came, must go home to die. He had been a man of some standing, rising fast in the State Department, and he had been suspicious of what his doctors told him, so he had asked them the brutal question brutally . . . A severe operation might save his life but afterwards there'd be painful treatment, he wouldn't be able to live a normal life; and the probability, almost the certainty, was further and even more desperate surgery.

Then how long? he had asked. They had hemmed and hawed for he was offending all their professional instincts, to say nothing of the chance of further fees. Finally a senior State Department official had bludgeoned them into reluctant estimate. Come clean or they were off his Department's list.

Six months.

So Wedder had come to the island for five of them. Mehmet Eldem considered he'd chosen well. Life in an institution for terminals wasn't one which any sane man would relish whereas here he would have his hobbies till he broke, sailing and swimming and soaking the sun up.

And of course he'd have Helen Withers too. Mehmet Eldem had learnt that quickly from the people on his list. Mostly they had been middle class people and such an open and wholly shameless liaison had offended their begrudging souls.

This morning he drove himself but with two armed men. Five Palestinians were inconveniently dead but there might well be others still at large. Mehmet had the soldier's philosophy without which no soldier could live and stay whole. If one came over with Mehmet's name on it that would be the end of Mehmet. But there was no point in taking unnecessary risks.

As he drove he considered what he could say to Wedder and what he could not. His General had spoken of some desperate last mischief by a PLO whose power was fading. Well, his General had been right: that had happened. Wedder's villa was only two miles from the mine and very probably he'd have heard the shooting, but he wouldn't know anything more than Mehmet did and to bring the subject up risked questions.

There were questions about that mine which mustn't be asked.

Mehmet drove fast on the coastal road for it carried military traffic and was well kept. But the tracks which led north to the beaches and villages were cracked and often deep in dust. He turned down the fourth or fifth and stopped suddenly. A hoopoe was taking a sunbath, wings spread, squatting in the dust in front of the car. He hooted but the bird didn't move: he began to inch forward but the hoopoe stood its ground. He said to one of the soldiers:

"Throw a stone. Be careful not to hit it, though."

The soldier found his stone and threw it, and the bird flew away with an arrogant squawk. The sunlight caught its superlative plumage. It was a pity, Mehmet Eldem reflected, that one of God's most beautiful creatures should smell like a neglected sewer.

They came to the village, entirely typical. There were a beach and a general shop, a small restaurant, a cluster of a dozen villas. Some were deserted and blackened shells for they'd belonged to Greeks and had been caught in the looting. Others had been spared or had been repaired. One stood untouched since a mainland Turk owned it. He had rented it to James Wedder for five months.

A car was in the road outside it – the doctor's probably, Mehmet guessed. He lit a cigar and waited patiently. Presently he felt stiff and got down, walking into the neat front garden. There were the usual things, hibiscus and cannas. The hibiscus seemed to be doing well but the cannas had gone back rather badly. If you didn't split the rhizomes they always did.

A woman came out of the house unexpectedly. He

had already paid her his duty call and had been courteously, rather coolly received. He had thought her face handsome if a trifle severe and she'd been wearing a housecoat which hid her figure. Today she was wearing a sweater and jeans and neither had come from a reach-me-down outfitter. Mehmet Eldem suppressed a mental wolf whistle. He had served three years in Europe proper but had retained his private tastes undiminished. He liked a woman to look like a woman. This one did.

"Good morning, Miss Withers."

"Good morning, Colonel Mehmet Eldem." That was what was engraved on his visiting card, his name and rank. Under it was written *Travellers Club* which he had happily joined in his time as a diplomat. He still belonged and hoped to use it again.

"All that is a bit of a mouthful, isn't it?"

He saw at once that he'd struck a false note. This woman was in no mood for banter; she was in fact in a towering rage. He changed gear with almost a diplomat's smoothness for his years amongst them had taught him to do so. "I came to see Mr. Wedder. How is he?"

She didn't answer at once but looked at him thoughtfully. What she saw was a man above middle height, dressed in English clothes and unquestionably male. He didn't look like any Turk she'd known, who were inclined to be bullet-headed and sallow. He might have been a man from the Midi. He stood easily on his feet and upright. A soldier, she thought: you could mostly talk straight to them.

"Mr. Wedder," she said, "is not in pain. But he would be if I didn't look after him."

"But surely the doctor – "

She made a small gesture of angry impatience. "I know you've been in England and know our ways but you can't be expected to spot the exceptions. Medical ethics are firmly established. Deliberately to take life is forbidden but if someone is suffering badly and terminal you may give him an increasing dosage which cumulatively you know to be fatal. That's the established practice and it's humane. But not here."

"May I ask – "

"Of course." Her rage was cooling but she was still very angry; she said at length: "Have you met the doctor?"

"He was on my list of people to call on."

"What did you make of him?"

Mehmet admired this woman's candour and wondered how far he could go to meet it. He decided on what was in fact a compromise. "I found him a trifle formal," he said.

"He's much worse than that, the man's a criminal. He has some sort of crazy religious conviction; he genuinely believes that suffering ennobles."

"Medicine and morality do not mix."

She looked at him again in surprise for she hadn't expected so black a wit. Both fell silent for both were thinking. He was thinking that this was a very nice woman and what she was doing was perfectly possible. There were a dozen open beaches they couldn't patrol. Contraband came in almost nightly and they hadn't the men to stem it effectively. It came in from mainland Greece and Crete, even from as far as Malta, run by families which had smuggled for centuries. There were drink and tobacco and even hard drugs. A legitimate analgesic was easy.

Just so long as it wasn't guns of any kind.

Helen's thinking had been a good deal shorter. She had decided that this man was civilised. She was confident enough of that but this was the moment to make perfectly sure. "And now I suppose you must try to stop me."

He didn't answer directly. "I was a soldier before they made me a lackey. I once gave a wounded man an overdose."

She held out her hand and he took it uncertainly. It occurred to him to kiss it gallantly but she was Lady

Withers' daughter – formidable. Instead he shook it gently and said: "Done."

He offered a cigarette and lit both. She was thinking again and Mehmet let her. Finally she said deliberately: "You have paid your duty call on me. Would you care to come again as a friend?"

"I'd like to very much indeed."

"Then come on Saturday at twelve for a drink."

He was surprised and said: "How do you know I sometimes drink?"

"James told me."

"I only drink with people I can trust."

"I take that as a compliment."

"It's a fact."

She said with a sort of stately archness: "And this time I shan't be wearing a housecoat."

He saw her into her car politely, then went into James Wedder's villa, walking through to the verandah at the back. Wedder was in a long cane chair. "Forgive me if I don't get up. I both sailed and swam this morning and it tired me."

Mehmet could see that this was sparing the truth. Wedder was legitimately tired but also he'd had an injection of morphia. He was in fact a little dopey but it didn't seem to have dulled his intelligence. "Take a shot," he said. "They're on the sideboard."

As he mixed one Mehmet asked gently: "So you told Helen Wither I occasionally drink?"

"Did I? Sometimes I don't remember too clearly – when I've had a heavy dose, I mean. I hope I haven't offended."

"No. But I'd like to know what you actually told her."

"I could only tell her what you'd told me. I said that you were solidly Sunni but not overly pious. Your grandfather was a friend of Atatürk. You believe in a God and you honour his Prophet but you won't have your daily life determined by priests. The fruit of the grape is specifically forbidden but it isn't the fruit of the grape which you fancy. I don't think I've ever seen you drink

30

wine. That little Jesuitry aside, you like gin. You never drink in public, never, and certainly not before other Muslims whom you'd offend."

"That's perfectly correct – you've done no harm. But I didn't come here to discuss your gin, or not to *discuss* in its common usage. I'm afraid I came to pick your brains."

"I haven't many left, you know."

"You were here *en poste* for six months and active. I know that that was some years ago, before the split, but Greeks haven't changed in six years nor six centuries."

"Nor are they likely to change in any way. Unlike the Israelis they'll forget a good turn but they'll pursue you to the death for tuppence."

"Which is exactly what they're trying to do now."

"You asked for my opinion: I give it. They haven't a hope of re-invasion."

"I think most sensible Greeks know that but they have other weapons and are using them cleverly. They're hitting our Achilles' heel – the economy."

"How?"

"By driving away the tourists for one thing, but they're also letting in men from Hezbollah and you know as well as I do what that's going to lead to sooner or later."

He was angling to discover how much Wedder knew but James Wedder went as dumb as a stone. To a professional diplomatist to let in Hezbollah was an action of unbelievable folly. In Lebanon a highly civilised state had been reduced to a bundle of warring cantons, six or seven militias slogging it out. To harbour such men could only be explained by malice. Greeks were a minor Balkan people, not seriously considered in Europe. This they knew and resented bitterly. So the temptation was to cock a snook. That they had apparently done and later they would repent it sadly.

James Wedder put the subject behind him; he was tired and preferred not to think about lunacy. Mehmet Eldem had felt on dangerous ground but Wedder moved away from it voluntarily. "Talking about driving away the tourists how do the saboteurs get in here to do it? The mountains are pretty closely patrolled and the plain has an electrified fence."

"They use the road which runs between them, the one which used to connect the two capitals."

"There's a United Nations control post on that."

"Which wouldn't stop a runaway dog. Its rules of engagement are simple and futile: they're never to shoot unless shot at first. And even if they were allowed to they wouldn't. Shooting would scare away a valuable perk."

"You mean they're venal?"

"Corrupt as hell. And it's interesting in its shameful way, a sort of microcosm of national character. The Indians take money quite naturally – there's an open and established tariff. If a havildar is in charge of the post it's a fiver a head for each man passing. A Lieutenant takes ten and a Captain twenty. The rare Major wants fifty and gets it."

"You've complained to the United Nations?"

"Of course not." Mehmet Eldem laughed contemptuously. "The United Nations is understandably touchy about the rabble it accepts as soldiers and this Province is not a member in any case."

"You could block the road below the picket, in territory you control *de facto*."

"We could but it might be counter-productive. Corruption has to be met by corruption and we've made our little arrangement too. The moment that picket has taken its bribe it rings us up and earns another. We don't catch everyone coming through – they scatter for their different targets – but we usually catch one at least and occasionally he knows something useful. When we've finished we push him back across the line. He hasn't a bruise or a scratch to complain of, quite often he remembers nothing, certainly not what he's actually told us. The days are happily past and gone when you filled a man up with pentathol and hoped that what he gabbled would be of use."

"So it's a balance of advantage and the reverse?"

32

"I suppose it is but it isn't a delicate one. If we effectively blocked that road, as we could, they'd simply come in through the open beaches. That wouldn't suit our book at all."

James Wedder said: "I suppose it wouldn't." He had been listening attentively but had noticeably tired. "I'll join you in that gin if you'll bring me one. It's an hour since I had that last injection."

"I thought you had to wait two at least."

"I'm supposed to and I usually do. But I'm in a position to accept risks happily." It was spoken without the least hint of self-pity.

When Mehmet returned with Wedder's drink he had moved from the chair to the open window. The morning breeze which made the summer heat tolerable had dropped. The last of it stirred the dusty back garden. Wedder had changed the subject; he said:

"You lead a very interesting life."

"My General's word for that was anomalous. I can't give orders to any soldier – the *Tuğgeneral* would drop on that – and I don't command the police directly. It's fortunate that I get on well with both but daily life is a bit of a tightrope."

"A tightrope is better than getting bored." James Wedder complained very seldom indeed, so seldom that Mehmet had listened uneasily. He liked James Wedder and greatly admired him; he hoped that he hadn't begun to break. But to talk for once might be helpful katharsis. "Please go on," Mehmet said.

"I've the swimming and the sailing still but I can't kid myself they'll go on for ever. 'Ever' meaning till I have to go home. I've re-read all of Trollope and enjoyed it. Helen comes to see me daily and behaves like the social worker she isn't. One or two friends come out as well and of those visits I value your own the most. But since I'm shamefully letting my hair down I'll let it fall. What I'm short of is really amusement. Regularly."

"I see you don't have a telly."

"It's rubbish."

"Then I might be able to help if only once."

Mehmet had made his decision quickly. This man was a friend and a friend of Turkey. He'd been posted here when the invasion had happened and he hadn't lost his head like some others. The diplomats as a whole had panicked and alarmist reports had gone home by the bagful. But James Wedder had seen it with a decent detachment. The Greeks, he had reported coolly, had really gone much too far for their own good. They had always treated the Turks rather badly but they'd recently launched a sort of pogrom. There'd been raids against non-existent cells of a Resistance the Turks were too weak to organise; there'd been detentions without trial and much worse. No doubt an invasion was entirely illegal but in human affairs the law wasn't everything. It was unfortunate that Turkish troops were largely armed from the American arsenal but the balance of power in the Mediterranean would not be disturbed if the North of this island were controlled by the people who mostly inhabited it. So make your disapproving noises but sit tight.

All this Mehmet knew and it tilted the balance. To discuss the raid he had thought impermissible but simply to take James Wedder to the mine would be a very much smaller risk if one at all. To visit it next Thursday at four o'clock. When an Israeli ship was due at the jetty, when interesting things were due to happen. Besides he was an intelligent man and had almost certainly made his guesses already.

Plain pyrites would be of no use to Israel.

Mehmet Eldem said again: "I might provide a moment's amusement. I'll call for you on Thursday at three o'clock."

*   *   *

Mehmet Eldem had had an early lunch since he'd arranged to meet James Wedder at three o'clock, and though the road was good there were also roadblocks.

34

They were manned half by police and half by soldiers and although they tried to be unobtrusive they were thorough and they took their time. He had put on service dress with a belt for he was taking James Wedder to visit the mine and the Major who commanded its guard had taken some trouble to stage his play, the black comedy which he hoped would amuse a friend. It was only polite to be properly dressed. He had taken an armed orderly with him but more as something which went with his uniform than from fear of any attack on his person. He drove himself.

He turned down the broken and dusty track which led to the sea and James Wedder's villa. The hoopoe was in the dust again but this time it flew away as the car came on; and again there was another car outside the house. There was a notice in the rear window: *Doctor on Duty*. Mehmet Eldem thought it distinctly pretentious.

The doctor had been on his General's list as a person who rated a formal call and Mehmet Eldem had therefore paid it. It had been stiffly received with a hint of patronage. Mehmet hadn't liked this German-Swiss and since Helen had told him his Calvinist credo was quite prepared to dislike him actively. He waited till the doctor came out, then got out of his car and walked up to him briskly. "Good afternoon, doctor."

"Good afternoon, Colonel." The rank was pronounced with a hint of distaste. This Swiss did not approve of the military.

"How is my friend your patient today?"

The doctor didn't relish the question which he considered was not for a layman in uniform. He's a pompous little fool, Mehmet thought, as well as an indifferent doctor. The doctor hesitated but finally spoke. This Colonel was an important man who could make trouble if he were openly rude.

"Mr. Wedder is not well, as you probably know, but his condition today is reasonably stable. However, that will not continue long if he persists in receiving treatment which I have not authorised."

35

To this harsh little sentence Mehmet said: "Yes?"

"Yes indeed. He is receiving drugs which I have not prescribed." The doctor looked at Mehmet hard. "I conceive you have the power to stop it."

"He is receiving some illegal drug – heroin or cocaine, for instance?"

"Not heroin or cocaine."

"Then what?"

"Morphia," the doctor said. "And too much of it."

"I doubt if that's widely used by addicts. I doubt if it's even illegal – formally."

"That may be so. It is quite irrelevant. But it is only obtainable on a doctor's prescription and Mr. Wedder is receiving more than I have prescribed. I repeat that it is your business to stop it."

Mehmet Eldem lost his temper but quietly. "I have seen this situation before. Something is being done which offends you and you're demanding I find some law to cover it."

"Good-day, Colonel."

"I wish you good-day."

The doctor drove away in his car and Mehmet took a minute to cool. Then he walked through the house to the back verandah.

Wedder rose from his long chair to greet him, something he didn't normally do. He moved easily and his eyes were bright. He said:

"You look very smart."

Mehmet Eldem was indeed very smart. Since he'd decided that this was an occasion for uniform he would dress properly or not at all. On his collar were his scarlet gorgets and a scarlet band round his brass-peaked cap. He wore a double-strapped black Sam Browne with elegance and, a Rifleman's sober privilege, the accoutrements were of solid silver. "I'm taking you to the mine," Mehmet said. "It's easier to get in like this."

"To the mine?" Wedder was clearly astonished. "I thought – "

"You thought correctly but I've brought you a pass."
He handed it over. "Now come with me."

At the guardhouse in the perimeter fence they were stopped and their passes examined meticulously. Neither was searched but the Colonel's car was. Finally the gates opened and they drove in. Just inside was the Major saluting rigidly. He too was wearing service dress for he too was feeling a sense of occasion. Mehmet said: "This is the friend I spoke of."

"Welcome, sir."

The Major got into the car with the driver and the four men drove to the mine's little landing pad. The pilot was at the controls but the blades were still. Normally men got in by a ladder but the Major had been carefully briefed and there was a portable set of steps for Wedder. They climbed in and the pilot started the engine. A cloud of red dust rose up and swallowed them but as the rotors bit on the heavy air they slowly began to climb above it. Quite soon they were clear and heading seawards.

They flew down the line of the overhead ropeway, watching it unroll below them. It was a formidable undertaking for a small mine for it ran from the pithead, sloping gently, till the ground levelled out to meet the sea. There were two hundred and fifty yards till the ropeway cleared the perimeter fence, then perhaps another hundred, dead flat, which ended at the head of a jetty. At it was moored a coastal freighter. Her hold was open to take the ore and she was flying a well-known flag of convenience. Once over her the helicopter turned, facing inland to watch the ropeway. There was a breeze off the land which was pushing her backwards and from time to time the pilot corrected. On the ropeway was a stream of hoppers but so far they hadn't begun to move. The watchers sat attentive, not speaking, the only sound the thud of the rotors.

Presently the hoppers moved, a string of ten bunched close together, a gap of thirty yards before one alone. As they came over the ship they opened and the ore fell into her hold with a crash. It had been dampened to minimise loss by dust. The ten hoppers dropped their loads and moved away, clanking round the return-gear noisily, disappearing on their long climb back to the pit. Then the single hopper came over the hold and dropped its load.

Unmistakably it was a plain pine coffin.

More hoppers followed and covered it decently, then another coffin and ten more of ore. The men in the chopper had counted five when the ship's siren gave a derisive hoot. Now the hoppers came down in a steady stream.

The chopper flew back to the mine and landed. The four men it carried were still in silence.

Driving back to James Wedder's villa Mehmet Eldem had watched him closely. He could see that his friend had been powerfully stimulated and he feared a sudden and unwelcome reaction. In the event his worry was wholly misplaced. Wedder went up the steps to his door as he'd gone up the steps to the chopper, ignoring them. Once inside the door he rang a bell and when his housekeeper appeared said firmly:

"Can you manage tea a bit early, please? And I'm hungry as a horse for once. Scones if you have them, otherwise plenty of buttered toast. And jam."

The housekeeper had produced all three and they were eating them at the dining-room table. Mehmet Eldem sat bolt upright since that was the way he'd been taught to sit by parents who'd been sticklers for table manners. James Wedder was relaxed and eating hard. He said on a note of what was almost apology:

"Excitement always gives me an appetite."

"It's something well known so eat away."

Mehmet had been watching James Wedder with an interest which he realised was clinical. This man had a quite extraordinary resilience. It was known that in the penultimate stages, before a man must go home to die, there could be enormous swings between good days and bad. This was clearly a very good day indeed and Mehmet was pleased to have been the proximate cause of it. But there was something else and he sensed it uneasily. Excitement did other things than whet appetites: it could loosen a man's tongue like alcohol. James Wedder was a New England American, reserved by nature and trained as a diplomat. Normally he would say nothing indiscreet. But he was suffering, if that was the word – he was suffering from an extreme of stimulus. Mehmet Eldem had taken a risk in administering it, confident that Wedder's nature and training would inhibit the desire to ask questions. The last thing Mehmet wanted was questions but James Wedder had swallowed a powerful drug. It was something which Mehmet had not foreseen. Now he would have to be very wary.

James Wedder took a fourth slice of toast, spreading butter on it carefully, then jam. His first question was entirely innocuous.

"What will the Israelis do with those coffins?"

"They'll probably think they are some sort of bomb, timed to blow up when the ship is in harbour. So they'll be opened with more than the usual care. When they find what's inside they'll give decent burial. It will hardly be with full military honours but they'll assume those five were Muslims and act accordingly. One of their too frequent boasts is that they respect the religions of other people."

"But they won't think it funny."

"I'm not so sure. Israelis have their own sense of humour and sometimes it's as black as night."

"And in any case they daren't make a fuss. They seem to need that pyrites too badly."

This was getting dangerous and Mehmet had decided his line. Against a man of Wedder's mental calibre verbal fencing would almost certainly fail. The thing to do was to throw him red herrings, fat and outrageously political fish which a man with James Wedder's background couldn't resist.

"I've often wondered. There's that country in Africa

39

with pyrites of all sorts and they're desperate to sell them to anyone who can pay. But they've annoyed the South Africans with futile threats and South Africa controls their routes to the sea. I find that a comforting thought, don't you?"

"There are parts of the United States where if you said that you'd be lynched on the spot."

Mehmet let his breath out softly. It seemed to be working. He went on smoothly.

"Or there's that railway to the sea which doesn't work. In my opinion it never will while Africans are trying to run it."

"In England you could get fined for that. Perhaps prison."

It was a second bait swallowed and Mehmet felt happier. The medicine of controversy seemed to be working and he decided to increase the dose. "We've no race relations problem here and therefore no clique to grow fat on exploiting it. We do have the ancient hatred of Greek for Turk but that goes back to the time of the Seljuks. Greeks think of Turks as barbarous blockheads and we think of them as obstreperous children who from time to time must be disciplined firmly. Which we do. Which causes more ill feeling in turn. Greeks are an intelligent people but one fatal mistake will always betray them. They sincerely believe that high intelligence is a substitute for the military virtues."

James Wedder laughed and Mehmet hid one. He was thinking that he had succeeded.

He had not. James Wedder said coolly: "That's provocative but I dare say you're right. What I don't see is how it bears on that mine. Greeks have their national characteristics and so have Israelis. But different. They're not conceited gamblers like the Greeks, they're shrewd and hard-headed businessmen. The mines across this Province's border are worked out: the yield is so low that nobody wants the ore." James Wedder leant forward, sharp-eyed and formidable. "Yet

40

a few miles away, within the Province, it's been worth your while to open a new one. And the Israelis, who don't make commercial mistakes, are buying up its output greedily. Now what do you make of that?"

"I don't." Mehmet realised that his ploy had failed and that Wedder was very close to the truth; he couldn't stop an intelligent man from adding two and two and making four but Wedder was behaving untypically; he might even ask a question directly and this Mehmet Eldem dare not answer. In a last attempt to duck he added:

"I'm not a mining engineer."

"Nor am I."

For a moment Mehmet thought he'd won after all. "Then let's leave it at that."

"By all means since we're neither of us experts. But one thing stands out like the proverbial sore thumb. The yield of that mine must be very rich."

Mehmet was obliged to admit it. "That's logical," he said reluctantly.

"Very, very, very rich."

The two men looked at each other in silence. Each knew that the other had guessed the truth. Both knew that neither would dare to utter it.

Mehmet went back to his office and made his report.

*   *   *

Mehmet Eldem had files on the Withers family and he decided he would refresh his memory before meeting Helen Withers again. They'd been left behind when the Greek police fled but the important ones had been translated carefully. Sir William had not been politically minded, at any rate between Greek and Turk, and it was hinted he thought his wife a fanatic. Indubitably she had been just that. As for the daughter she had been only a girl. She sometimes came down to the

41

villa on holiday and later had come in her long vacations. The assessment was short and quite close to dismissive.

A pleasant young woman and apparently disinterested. She now teaches at a women's college and appears to be a little innocent.

Mehmet put the file down and laughed. For one thing Helen wasn't innocent: he didn't think she'd been sweet-and-twenty since several years before that birthday. But it was a typical piece of Greek folly to think so. Politically they were indecently clever but when it came to people made stupid mistakes.

There was nothing else on her file of interest and he put it down and turned to her mother's. It had been compiled by Greeks and was therefore hostile but the story was there and Mehmet read it again. It was the story of a remarkable woman and of a desperate time in the island's long history. Knowing something of those decisive years, contemporary events made some sense.

William Withers had been a talented chemist in an establishment in darkest Wiltshire. The government insisted loudly that it had nothing to do with chemical warfare: all it did was to make protective clothing. Few people were interested and even fewer believed it but it was a convenient front for a shaky government beset by the *bons penseurs* beyond its pale. William Withers had not been Sir William then but he'd been climbing and had been sent to a conference. Amsterdam he had thought a shabby city but Agnes van der Bijl the opposite. A month later she had known she was pregnant.

Very un-Dutch but they'd both been young.

Her family had been influential and William Withers quietly ambitious. Maybe they couldn't have broken him finally but they could put his career back by several years. They'd held the gun, William Withers had bowed to it.

Mehmet laughed again as he read steadily on. How

42

that Withers had carried the whole thing off! To a shotgun marriage you took your Purdey, not some miserable pumpgun made in Belgium. He had arrived in Amsterdam in style, with a Bentley which he happened to own and a manservant whom he'd temporarily hired, and he'd put up in a suite in the Doelen hotel. He could afford all three since he was comfortably off. Then he'd telephoned to the father politely. The marriage, he understood, was at noon so he'd arrive at the church at a quarter to. Yes, he'd be suitably dressed and attended. He'd remembered to bring a best man too.

Then he'd driven her off on a formal honeymoon and on it he had fallen in love with her. Not that that had solved all problems for she hadn't liked England, or not life in Wiltshire. They'd had a comfortable flat in the guarded Establishment but Establishment life she had found intolerable, the endless jockeying and the bitchy women. So why didn't she go and live on that island, the island where they'd spent their honeymoon? He had his work which she knew absorbed him, and he'd visit her every six weeks at most. Their married life had been a series of honeymoons.

And in the intervals she hadn't been bored for she'd acquired a passionate political interest. She was northern Dutch, injustice offended her, and the Turks around her were vilely treated. You didn't need sociological training to see that they were third class citizens; they did most of the menial work and were badly paid; if a crime was committed a Turk was arrested first and beaten. Protestant Agnes Withers had been outraged. There was a powerful Greek lobby in the United States but nobody to speak for poor Turks. At first her task had been hard and fruitless, trying to get other expatriates interested, writing letters to the English newspapers which as often as not they didn't publish.

And then one day she had had her first success. She had taught herself to speak fluent Turkish and had heard hundreds of complaints of maltreatment. This old man had been dispossessed of his land on a legal fiddle the

43

Greek courts had upheld. That happened every week of the year and there wasn't any normal remedy. When he'd protested they'd followed the established routine; they had cooked up a charge and put him in prison, and in prison he'd been brutally beaten.

A commonplace tale and she'd heard it a dozen times but this time the story was backed by real evidence. She had gone to a young lawyer she knew, a rising star who by now was the Man – no less. He had grabbed at the case with eager hands. He'd been a Deputy, too, and had political connections. Moreover he was good at publicity; he had blown the thing up into a sort of State Trial. Other countries had sent their best reporters. The trial had become a red hot story.

Finally he had won his case.

By now Agnes was a local heroine, or she was to the grateful Turkish community. To the Greek establishment she was simply anathema. Things began to go wrong in her house. Her Greek servants disappeared without warning. She took in Turks and trained them patiently. There were a couple of fires and a minor burglary and one day the boiler blew up mysteriously. There was even an open move to expel her, an approach to the British High Commission that she'd been meddling in local politics and was no longer *persona grata* as a guest. The High Commissioner was as wet as the next one but Agnes was Lady Withers now and her husband a man of increasing importance. It had gone against the grain to do so but he'd plucked up what was left of his manhood and told the official who'd called to get lost. The pinpricks had gone on unabated but Agnes Withers had stuck it out stubbornly.

Or she had until one day the lawyer called on her. She could see that he was badly frightened but also that it was not for himself . . . There were going to be untoward events and her house was very near the main beach. She would be wise to go away for a bit.

Like hell, she would. She would stay and she'd help.

44

The lawyer who was now the Man had looked doubtful but he would pass on her message.

Ten days later a Turk had rung her bell. He was dressed in a labourer's clothes and was scruffy but he spoke educated Turkish crisply . . . Had she by any chance work for a poor man? Weeding the garden – anything. She had told him to go to the servants and ask. At least they would give him a proper meal.

Five minutes later he'd been sitting in her drawing room. He'd introduced himself as *Binbaşi*, a Major, and he'd been brief.

He understood she had made an offer.

She had.

In that case she could do his country a service. She had friends all over the island and a car. She could go where she liked without raising suspicion and also she was fond of walking. Naturally she preferred to walk off the roads.

That, she had said, was so. Please go on.

He had produced a marked map and spread it carefully. The circles were where the Greeks kept their soldiers for they didn't maintain a central garrison. It was realised she hadn't been trained in espionage but nothing was being asked that she couldn't do. It was vital to know troop movements in advance, roughly how many men and in which direction. He had given her a radio and a simple word-code in which to communicate. It was never to be carried with her but hidden in her house with great care. She was to use it at two fixed times and no other, when it would be comparatively safe to do so. Finally he had produced a document. She had been surprised and had asked what it was.

"It is a commission in the Turkish army. Madam, you are now a Lieutenant."

She had said with immediate indignation: "I'm not working for you for money, you know."

"I know that well – you miss the point. But the fact that you were a regular officer might help you if you were ever captured. The Greeks have some disagreeable habits with people who they suspect are spies."

She'd been taken once but they'd let her go, a picket a mile from one of the camps. They had searched her but she'd been clean of suspicion – no fieldglasses and of course no map. She'd been wearing heavy walking boots and carrying a walker's pack. She'd been some way from any restricted area and she'd protested in highly colloquial English. The picket's sergeant had let her go.

It had proved a very expensive mistake for Agnes Withers was quick and observant, and she hadn't made the amateur's error of crowding the air with irrelevant trifles. When she had something hot she sent it and when she had not she kept radio silence.

The Turks had come in on a minor beach, two miles from where the Greeks had expected them. And they'd made Lady Withers the Colonel-in-Chief of a highly respected Turkish regiment.

Mehmet Eldem put the file away thoughtfully. His General had been perfectly right. If this woman's daughter were in any way troubled his army's honour would be down in the dust. He'd learnt little of fact which he didn't know but he'd learnt something else of the greatest importance. With the parentage she undoubtedly had Helen Withers would have very strong genes. In vulgar but permissible terms she'd be as stubborn as a Missouri mule.

He arrived at her house at twelve precisely, stopping in the street outside to admire its soberly decent proportions. It wasn't a box on a beach like James Wedder's but a solid town house several streets from the sea. There was no garden in front but a handsome doorcase. At the back would be the servants' quarters.

A young manservant opened the door to his knock. He was wearing a white housecoat with a stiff-looking military collar, hooked. He had clearly been warned of Mehmet's visit and said respectfully:

"Good morning, Pasha."

46

"I'm afraid I'm not a Pasha yet."

The youth flushed and said something in local Greek, then returned to the little English he knew. "Please to come in, sir. I'll show you up." He led Mehmet upstairs and knocked on a door. When Helen's voice answered he threw it open; he announced Colonel Mehmet Eldem and withdrew.

Mehmet took two paces forward and stopped dead.

Helen Withers had had no files to refer to – she'd been thinking hard. She'd been attracted by this personable soldier and James Wedder hadn't long to live. The Almighty in His infinite wisdom had made her in the form He had chosen and this she had accepted happily. But Mehmet Eldem came from a different culture and she couldn't be sure how he'd read her signals. So she wouldn't give him an outright come-on but she'd give him a deliberate tease. He might be one of those prudish Muslims who took umbrage if a woman painted her face and more than mere umbrage if she flaunted her blessings. On the other hand he might be less civilised than he appeared. In which case he would probably rush her. If that happened she would submit to him graciously but she wanted something more than that from this intelligent and interesting male.

Mehmet had stopped as though he'd been shot but now came on. Helen was standing bolt upright, motionless, holding a conscious pose. When he'd seen her last she'd been wearing jeans but today's were a good deal tighter and smarter. Her linen had not been cut for comfort. She looked like a generously graven caryatid but a caryatid dressed up to kill. Her black hair was in a single pigtail and her face was made up to the edge of vulgarity. She hadn't gone over that edge but she'd come close. Round her neck she wore a choker of pearls. "Sit down," she said, "and I'll get you that promised drink."

Mehmet was glad to sit down for he needed to think fast. He wasn't without experience and this wasn't a common or garden green light. When she'd come to the island before she had come with men and she hadn't any need to bait her hook. No, this was a test of himself, quite deliberate, and a lot would depend on how he handled it.

She brought him a drink but not one for herself. "Aren't you drinking?" he asked.

"At half-past twelve and it isn't that yet. I'm as fond of gin as the next man or woman but if I drink too much I put on weight."

"It would be a pity," he said, "to spoil perfection."

This earned him the expected smile. "You really speak remarkable English."

"And so I should. I was in England two years, attached to my embassy. I was a Military Attaché, you see, which in practice means a tolerated spy. But I mixed with other diplomats and whatever their numerous failings may be diplomats tend to speak passable English. There is also another and pleasanter method of learning to speak a language properly."

"No doubt," she said. "You don't disappoint me."

So far, he was thinking, it has gone rather well but her next question threw him back on his heels. "How's the Gestapo this morning?" she asked.

He was shaken and took his time to recover. This wasn't the sort of question conventionally asked. He decided it was another fly and this time he wouldn't gobble it greedily. He said without offence but firmly:

"The Gestapo was mostly low class Bavarians officered by sadistic aristocrats. I'm not an aristocrat and I'm not a yobbo. I'm a Turk of a respectable family."

How easy it was, she was thinking privately, to get a man to tell you his background. But she saw that she'd taken this one too lightly. He was saying with a smile which half mocked her:

"You could have asked me that outright – I'd have told you. Now I've given you something and I want something back. Don't tell me about your mother – I know all that. Tell me about yourself, what you do."

"I teach classics at Oxford. St. Mildred's College. You've heard of it?"

"Indeed I have."

"Then I needn't bore you."

He took time to reflect on St. Mildred's College for one of his English girlfriends had been there. She'd been a simple, generous-hearted girl and St. Mildred's rather stuffy aura hadn't suited her pagan spirit at all.

It was bitterly nonconformist and serious; it deprecated all carnal pleasure; it was harsh to its students and proud to be dull.

Mehmet returned to the present and Helen. "I'm surprised you chose St. Mildred's," he said.

"So was mother but it all happened naturally. I liked classics at school and I suppose I was good at them because St. Mildred's gave me an open scholarship. I worked hard since there wasn't much else to do at St. Mildred's and I managed to scrape a First. They took me on. I'm what is called a junior lecturer."

"Do you like it?" he enquired.

"Yes and no. There are generous holidays which I spend down here, making up for lost time which I haven't quite done yet. And I genuinely enjoy the teaching. I suppose it's the thing I do best, come to that."

He doubted it but didn't say so.

She looked at her watch. "It's half-past twelve. Get me that drink, please. Lemon with it but no ice. Ice with everything is an American cliché."

He mixed the drink with proper care but she could see that it didn't absorb him entirely. On the wall above the row of bottles was an abstract which he had looked at with interest. When he brought her the drink she asked him quietly:

"Tell me what you think of my picture."

"I didn't have time to look at it properly."

"Then let's have another look." They both got up. She stood beside him, too close for his comfort. "Well?"

He said on a note of casual irony which she noticed and marked him up for highly: "Turks aren't supposed to know much about the arts."

"I can't think why not. You have some classic miniaturists and some beautiful rugs. A really good Bergamo can stare down most of what comes from Persia."

"I cannot paint nor weave a knot."

"You're stalling," she said. "What about that picture?"

"Whoever painted that was in mental pain." He hesitated but brought it out. "I think he was trying to escape from something. I don't know from what but he was on the run."

She was as astonished as he himself had been when he'd first come into this handsome room. Words like 'sensitive' were nowadays pejorative and in any case were not to be uttered. But there was more to this man than a fine pair of shoulders.

"It's a Picasso," she said, "or maybe it isn't."

They had sat down again and she went on coolly. "Mother saw it in an art dealer's window in Amsterdam. But the great man was there too, for an exhibition, and when he saw it he promptly disowned it. No, it wasn't a copy, it was an impertinent fake. But he did paint a shocking lot, you know, and by the time he saw that picture there he was as near to gaga as made no difference. There are respectable and learned experts who are still prepared to swear it's genuine. But when the old man disowned it and threw a tantrum naturally the price dropped to nothing. Mother paid two hundred pounds. But in maybe five years or maybe ten, while the experts have been quietly beavering, when an old man's anger is long forgotten, it might be worth a lot of money. But painters go in and out of fashion for no reason a layman can easily follow and Picasso painted a flock of potboilers."

"You've insured it, of course?"

"I can't do that. No company will insure a fake."

"But you hang it on a wall in your house."

"Why not? I like it and it's there to look at. The alternative is some vault in a bank."

He nodded but in turn didn't speak for like Helen he held some things unutterable. He would have liked to say but did not dare that he thought this a civilised thing to do.

Helen Withers changed the subject smoothly. "Do you mind if we go back to St. Mildred's?"

In fact he did; he was bored by St. Mildred's. She saw his face change and said at once: "Not about the College – about me." She gave him a cool but friendly smile. "After all you did ask for information."

"Go on."

"I'm in some trouble with St. Mildred's College."

They were relaxed by now, on established terms, and he saw no point in beating about the bush. "About James?" he asked.

"Again yes and no. They know I have mother's house down here and I dare say they've heard gossip about James. But as long as I keep my nose clean in Oxford there's little they can do about that. If they sacked me for a discreet affair I could sue them and very probably win. In any case they wouldn't do it. It would strike them as illiberal and at St. Mildred's that's a very bad word."

"Then what's the trouble?"

"It's one of time. I'm on a three-year contract to teach in termtime and if I break it they can legitimately fire me. The long vacation is nearly finished and to put it crudely James Wedder isn't. I'm not a don and I don't have tenure."

"You could ask for special leave."

"I have. They said they would consider it carefully."

"May I ask an indiscreet question?"

"I'll risk it."

"How long do you think James Wedder has to go?"

Helen Withers didn't answer directly. "I've been trying to get him to move in here. But apart from that almost compulsive reading all he has is the sea and a boat to sail in. This house is half a mile from a beach, and though

51

he could keep his boat in the harbour it's crowded and a mile at least."

"May I ask a last question?"

Helen nodded.

"When his time comes to go home, to hospital, will you go too?"

"I would if he asked me but he's far too considerate. The last fortnight or two can be pretty traumatic. I had an uncle by marriage who died of cancer and at the end he didn't know his own wife."

"And meanwhile if St. Mildred's gets nasty?"

"St. Mildred's," she said, "can go to hell."

"You're a very nice woman."

She took it smiling. "I hope to convince you shortly that I am not." She rose and Mehmet Eldem rose with her. "I'm sorry I can't ask you to lunch. It's cook's day off – I'll have to do for myself."

It occurred to him again to kiss her hand but Helen might think the gesture affected and he wasn't a Latin to do it naturally. Instead he said:

"I must see you again."

"Ask me to dinner next week."

"It's done."

He walked home thoughtfully, not displeased. He hadn't believed the story about the cook. She was timing the affair fastidiously. For affair there was going to be – that was certain. But if she wasn't rushing it nor was he.

*   *   *

The meeting was held in the Bishop's palace which the bishop had incontinently abandoned along with the other Greek bigwigs who had fled. It was now the Man's makeshift headquarters, supported by several neighbouring villas. But these had all been pressed into service, not sequestrated – the Man was always insistent on that. No Greek title had been overridden. Did some Turk now farm what had once been Greek acres? Then he paid a proper rent for them to an official called the

Custodian General as the Man paid him rent for this cluster of buildings. The South would not accept these moneys, preferring to keep refugees on the breadline as an example of Turkish contempt for law when it privately knew that this wasn't the case. After all, it had an established precedent. There were rich Arab states which let men fester in camps for reasons which were purely political. The Man was not disturbed by this. These payments were increasing daily and would one day be an important counter in the bargaining which he believed was inevitable. His policy was to hang on, keep his head down. He was in *de facto* control of a considerable territory, and although the Province had several problems, chief of them a shortage of money, he was holding it together effectively. One day the world would get tired of Greek protests; one day world opinion would swing his way.

Meanwhile he made the most of what he had. This wasn't a lot but somehow he managed. The civil service had been mostly Greek and this had gone. That the Man could bear with fortitude for it had been overstaffed and lazy and venal. The shortage of police was much more serious but there were Turkish soldiers whose time was expiring and who were happy to take steady work as policemen. What really bit was the lack of administrators. A few Turks had been members of what had once been the parliament but only one other beside himself had been allowed by the Greeks to run a Department. Again the Man was not overly worried. Provided a Turk could patch and mend, take sensible decisions quickly, parliamentary experience was now irrelevant.

The Man walked to the window and looked down at the garden. Once it had been discreetly impressive with statues which were perhaps surprising for a prelate who was supposed to be celibate but now these had gone and the lawn they had stared at was covered by temporary buildings of all sorts. In one of them was Mehmet's modest office. His staff was small for it had been kept so deliberately. The last thing the shrewd General had wanted was to give the impression that a third power was operating.

The Man went back to his table and looked at a clock. There were five minutes still to the time of the meeting and he spent them in not too dissatisfied thought.

For he was pleased with Mehmet Eldem and with reason. The Brigadier who commanded the garrison was prickly; it would have been easy to upset him seriously but Mehmet had deferred to him pointedly, always calling him 'Sir' and never 'Brigadier'. And the Chief of Police he had handled tactfully. He'd been an Inspector and under Greek rule would have stayed one. Unless, of course, he could have found the large sum which would have been necessary to buy him promotion. He was earthy and tough but he was also a stopgap. Mehmet Eldem got along with him beautifully. The Man could recognise worldly skills.

When the intercom rang he said: "Show them in, please," and rose and walked to a switch on the wall. Two overhead fans had been turning lazily but now he turned them up to full. He wouldn't have air-conditioning at any price. He didn't believe that it made a man impotent but he did believe that it made him infertile.

Three men came in and were given chairs, the Brigadier, the Chief of Police and Mehmet. A servant brought them the ritual coffee and while they drank it Mehmet looked round the room. He had seen the Man several times by now but always in his personal office, a much smaller room on a lower floor. This one had been the bishop's study and Mehmet took it in approvingly. It was a fine, high room with a coffered ceiling and most of the walls were covered with bookcases. The books in them were expensively bound. In the open spaces was a collection of icons which Mehmet could see were both old and good, certainly not the local daubs which monks had once painted for credulous tourists, darkening their gaudy colours by holding them in front

54

of wood fires. The Man was pious in an orthodox way and Mehmet Eldem was mildly surprised that he'd kept these very Christian symbols. But this was a private room after all, not a place where they would offend the faithful.

The Man tapped the table lightly and said: "The Brigadier to speak first, if you please."

The Brigadier cleared his throat ceremonially; he had prepared what he wanted to say and said it. "That attack on the mine will not be repeated, or not in the same way as before. The mountain patrols have been reinforced and there's a permanent picket on the top of that cliff. In passing, there's a body at its foot. It's lying in what is surely Greek territory so naturally we haven't been down there. Some sort of guide, I suppose, whom the raiders dumped. Which brings me to another aspect, another reason for modest confidence that the mine will not be attacked again. Or not yet. Those five we shot were Palestinians and in the world of the Palestinian terrorist expert climbers do not grow on trees. Not that that solves our immediate problem which is these raids across our border against the hotels."

"Can you do anything to minimise that?"

"I have. I've put a roadblock down on our side of the border, a hundred yards below those useless UN."

The Man frowned slightly for he didn't much like it. "That might be a breach of the ceasefire terms and will certainly give a lot of offence. The last thing in the world we want is to give the South a real cause for complaint. Their Public Relations is much slicker than ours. You've blocked one way in but not the other. It forces them to come in by sea."

"And the 'them'," the Chief of Police said quietly, "is going to be something different in future."

"This is something new?"

"I'm afraid it is."

"Then I'd very much prefer to have it straight."

The Chief of Police was a cautious man and he began

on a note of deprecation. "You mustn't think I'm a sort of spymaster with a fully organised network down in the Greek South. But there are Turks who stayed there as some Greeks stayed here and many of them cooperate gladly. I do get information – quite a lot. No doubt the Brigadier does too."

The *Tuğgeneral* said a little stiffly: "I am interested in Greek troop movements and even more interested in the extent to which the ceasefire levels are being broken. Greek soldiers are being smuggled in daily, often with rather more than their sidearms. They come in as civilians and are next seen in barracks. But military Intelligence doesn't clash with civilian."

Mehmet Eldem was delighted to hear it for if true it was entirely exceptional. His time in the West had impressed on him firmly that where there was more than one source of Intelligence disaster followed as night followed day.

The Man turned back to the Chief of Police. "Then tell us what your sources tell you."

"The Palestinian rump is licking its wounds, which is not to say that it won't recover or return in a much more dangerous form. As I said, the present danger is something new. So far we've had to deal with small fry, people who made the hotels unsafe and kept them at the best half full. The South did not discourage them but they weren't their men. Now they are. In future we shall have to deal with professionals."

"Professional thieves?"

"No, professional terrorists."

"Explain," the Man said.

"I will do my best." The Chief drew a breath and then spaced his words carefully. "The government of the South is now in this directly. It has been sending its own men for training, not Palestinians but its own Greek subjects."

"Training in what?"

"In a single word – terrorism. They won't be up to the highest standards but they'll be fertile soil for the nastier

56

tricks of the trade. Even mainland Greeks despise the locals."

The Man thought this an exaggeration, the sort of knee-jerk reaction he deplored, but he passed it without the reproof he felt it deserved; he had decisions to make and asked instead:

"You're sure of this?"

"There is excellent evidence. Even a small camp where these terrorists live."

"How many are there?"

"Naturally the estimates vary. An average would be twenty-five."

"And how are they going to get in?"

"By sea. Our northern coast is quite indefensible."

All four men fell grimly silent for all of them were obliged to accept it. It had often been discussed before and always without a useful result. There were a dozen open beaches spread widely and many things came across them quite freely. As James Wedder and Helen, Mehmet thought, have very good reason to know and bless. Counter-measures had been discussed and turned down. There wasn't the manpower to seal the beaches and reinforcements were politically out. Then put a man on each beach with a radio? Pointless. By the time a patrol could arrive to support him the terrorist would have done his job, slipping away by another beach. And the problem went far beyond open beaches. An inflatable from a ship could land anywhere, even swimmers if they'd been taught to do so. As they would have been and Mehmet guessed where.

He grunted in an angry frustration. The Man's policy was to play it long and Mehmet Eldem shared his opinion that this was right. To ask for another battalion of troops would be to give the Greeks a head on a plate and they could be trusted to make an enormous meal of it. And if you brought in that battalion secretly, in dribs and drabs as the South was doing, it would be months before it was up to strength and capable

57

of controlling the coast. In any case, Mehmet Eldem decided, the problem wasn't really military: it was a problem of having the navy the Province had not. Sowing mines might be possible but that would endanger the local cabotage. Two old gunboats had been found in the harbour. They hadn't even challenged the landings; they were obsolete and slow and scrap iron. What was wanted was fast patrol boats. There were none.

The Man brought them back from unhappy reflection with another soft tap on the bishop's fine table. "Very well," he said, "so they come in by sea. What is going to be their target?"

"People," the Chief said. "They're terrorists." He was gaining in self-confidence as he sensed he was gaining the others' respect. "The hotel angle is almost played out. The tougher regulars are drifting back and the hotels have recruited their own protection." He indulged a rare policeman's smile and added: "Some of it is a good deal rougher than we should ever dare to be."

"Very well then, they go for people. What people?"

"The residents, the expatriate community. If we should lose that we'd be close to bankruptcy."

The Man nodded briefly for he knew it was true. Visitors brought money in but the resident foreigners were a standing asset and its loss would be a serious blow. The Man said at length: "They can't go for all of them."

"I'm afraid they don't need to. What they'll be after will be a state of panic. One or two spectaculars . . ."

"Killings?"

"With the utmost brutality."

"It's barbarous," the Man said angrily.

"Remember these men have been trained by Arabs."

The Man looked at the Brigadier, then at Mehmet. "You think this is on?"

"I'm afraid I do." The Brigadier had spoken first. "It isn't too hard to induce a panic. Look at what happened here a few years ago. Thousands of Greeks left the Province who needn't have."

"Colonel Eldem?"

Mehmet Eldem nodded.

The Man turned back to the Chief of Police. "Then what are we going to do?"

"What we can. Which isn't very much, I'm afraid. We're on the defensive again – like guarding the coast, or rather not guarding it. A police patrol drives through the town every night, and if it happens to meet an incident it can intervene. But there's no guarantee it will see a thing."

"Just the one patrol? That sounds pretty thin."

"I can raise it to two in a few days' time. Ten policemen are coming out of the training school, and though they won't be fit for patrolling they'll release ten other men who are."

"Blind patrolling in a town is a waste of time." It was the Brigadier and a little patronising.

The Chief of Police took it amiably. "Just so, sir. A patrol needs to know the probable targets. So I have made a little list." He passed it round the table and waited.

Mehmet Eldem looked at his copy with interest. It was shorter than his General's list but that had been one of people to call on, people who might give him the smell of things. But this was a list of *prominenti*, persons whose murder might start a panic, the general exodus which would bankrupt the Province.

The Man began to read from it thoughtfully. "I see that His Highness comes first," he said. "He's by far the richest man in the Province."

"With great respect, sir, money isn't the point. If these terrorists see anything easy to steal, gold plate, for instance, or maybe money, they'll probably pick it up on the way. But unlike the small fry we've had before their object isn't stealing but murder. The murder of our most eminent resident would be a feather in their cap to boast of."

"They'd find it pretty hard," Mehmet said. "His Highness has a guard of his own and with your permission it's also armed. They're tough Punjabi Muslims, ex-soldiers, and moreover they owe him a feudal allegiance. They have eaten his salt and would die for him dutifully."

"You have a valid point but not a complete one. Ex-regular soldiers aren't trained against terrorists. However . . ." The Man looked down at the list again. "So Number Two, the Baron von Ems, the much publicised German financial tycoon."

The Brigadier said: "He isn't here."

"I know perfectly well he isn't here." It was said with a certain irritation. "But his villa is always fully manned and he arrives as he pleases without giving notice. Moreover he arrives in some state – his own aeroplane – and he brings with him a considerable retinue. His arrival couldn't be hidden for an hour." The Man looked at Mehmet Eldem and asked: "How does that seem to you?"

"Improbable. There'll be some valuable things in the Baron's villa but we're agreed that these men aren't common thieves. They might kill him as easily as anybody else but he wouldn't be my own choice as a target. Most of the residents here are British and he isn't, well, he's not representative."

"Then who would you first go for yourself?"

"Old Maurice Fazakerly."

There was a moment of laughter but it wasn't contemptuous. Fazakerly was getting on; he was pompous and boring, often intolerable; but he was also a very long way from gaga and something of a father figure.

"And he's President of the Club," the Brigadier said.

"Which opens another unwelcome line of thought. They could go for the institutions, not the men. I only know two, the church and that Club." The Man turned again to Mehmet Eldem. "You're the newest here and therefore the freshest. Tell us what you think of that."

"I doubt if the church is in danger – it's moribund. An Anglican priest in retirement looks after it and the

English make his pension up by passing round the community hat. If terrorists burnt his church to the ground I doubt if the English would build another. But the British Club is another story. Not all of them use it every day and some of them hardly go at all but it continues as a sort of symbol. I've heard it called a corporate identity."

"That was interesting but in a sense a digression." The Man looked down at the paper before him. "For we still have another name on the list, Miss Helen Withers." He looked sharply at the Chief of Police. "Elucidate, please," he said. "We can all of us guess but we'd better hear it."

"Miss Withers isn't permanently resident. She is no doubt comfortably off but she isn't rich. She isn't in any social sense prominent. She doesn't belong to the British Club, indeed most of the British disapprove of her strongly. But the murder of Lady Withers' daughter would shake them as it would surely shame us."

"Very well put," the Man said. "Very neat."

"Permission to speak, sir?" the Brigadier asked. He had been commissioned from the ranks and still said that.

The Man would have liked to laugh but didn't. Instead he said smoothly: "Granted gladly."

"Blind patrolling, as somebody said, is a waste of time but I'm prepared to put two men on Miss Withers' house."

"Thank you, Brigadier. I'm grateful. Then I think that concludes the morning's business." He had started to rise when the Chief of Police checked him. His budding confidence was now full blown.

"I should like to make a point for the record."

"Yes?"

"I shouldn't like to be misunderstood. I said that the Arab refugees were quiescent. I meant by that what's left of the PLO in the South. But a very different brand is filtering in."

"You mean Hezbollah?"

The Chief of Police nodded.

61

"You do well to remind us. The point is taken." The Man stood up with an air of finality. "Thank you, gentlemen, that is all for this morning. The best of luck to you in your different duties."

And by God, he was thinking, you're going to need it.

Mehmet Eldem walked back to his office thoughtfully. When in London he'd gone to theatres keenly but the entertainment he liked had been hard to find. What he liked was the well made three-act play and if such a thing were put on at all the critics promptly beat it into the ground. They would stand for slack craftmanship, obscene dialogue (which they excused with the popular buzzword 'freshness'), provided the play had a social message. Another buzzword whose meaning was wholly subjective.

So the critics would scarcely deign to notice what was happening on this divided island. For this was the quintessential three-act play. First the attack on the mine by the PLO, something to grip the audience quickly, then the development act which was still on stage, an undeclared war between Greek and Turk. The third would involve the Arabs again, not the discredited rump of the PLO but something newer and much more dangerous. The General had taken Hezbollah seriously.

Who had no interest in bankrupting Turks directly but whose enemy was always Israel. And there was a mine in this Turkish-backed breakaway Province which was clearly of great importance to Israel. Yes, the Chief of Police had done well to remind them all. The second act of this play was local Greek against Turk but the final act would be international.

Mehmet completed the walk to his office. It had been kept small deliberately, as unobtrusive as possible. On the door was a board with his name and rank but no legend to describe his duties. Inside was a staff of just four men, a Captain who was a trained interrogator and who also handled such cyphering as was necessary, two orderlies and a telegraphist for the radio.

He had gone to his modest room and sat down, prepared to consider the morning's meeting in detail, when the Staff Captain came in and saluted correctly. "A message from the General," he said, "I have decyphered it." He handed it over.

Report received. Stop. Sincere congratulations considerable coup. Stop. Convey my regards to Lady Withers' daughter. Ends.

"You've acknowledged this?"

"Yessir."

"And destroyed the working?"

"Of course, sir." The Staff Captain was a little offended.

"Then this can go on the record *en clair*."

Mehmet settled to thought again but not now about the morning's meeting . . . *"Lady Withers' daughter"* – an odd way to put it. And the General had admitted he'd known Agnes Withers well. He'd been commanding a Brigade of infantry when the Turkish troops had stormed the beaches, and one of Lady Withers' titbits had been news that Greek armour, such as it was, had not been moved down from the capital to the coast. If it had been it could have savaged infantry which was landing with little more than its sidearms; and by the time the Turks had their armour ashore there'd been no point in fighting an armoured battle. Turkish armour was both newer and heavier. No wonder that Turkish infantry regarded Agnes Withers as their Saint Joan.

And of course she had often been living alone when Sir William was not on one of their honeymoons.

It was an interesting speculation but Mehmet Eldem suppressed it reluctantly. Another line of thought had struck him, less interesting and a little disturbing. For he was conscious of a dereliction of duty – not a serious one but still dereliction. He'd been too interested in Helen Withers herself to think much about Lady Withers' daughter. Who, if the Chief of Police was right, was

63

a tempting target for terrorist murderers quite apart from the sterile Greek lust for revenge.

Mehmet decided he'd been given a warning. It was oblique, perhaps, but no less forceful for that. If anything happened to Helen Withers the head of Mehmet Eldem would roll.

So be it, then – he'd start tomorrow. He was going to give her dinner at Nico's.

* * *

Mehmet Eldem had waited ten days before inviting Helen to dinner. She was setting the pace to an inevitable finish and he was perfectly content to let her. But when he did ring he was precise and firm. No "One day next week" but "Thursday evening."

"I'd like to but on one condition. Not at The Grapevine – it stinks to heaven." She parodied The Grapevine's chi-chi menu. "'Prime Scottish beef from the misty Highlands marinated for days in our own preparation of herbs. Garden fresh peas with the scent of the dawn on them.'"

He laughed in quick appreciation for her sense of humour could be as acid as his own and that would be an important asset in whatever the future held for both of them. "When I was in London there were dozens of those, mostly down the Fulham Road. I gather they're now very dead indeed. No, I was going to take you to Nico's."

"But Nico's is Greek."

"Of course it's Greek, and what of that? Nico keeps his head down politically so he's perfectly free to run a restaurant. As it happens it's the best on the island and that includes the flashy ones down in the South. Do you like lamb?"

"Lamb isn't in season."

"It is in the real mountains still."

"Which aren't in the Province."

"I could still get you lamb."

64

It was Helen Withers' turn to laugh. "So the spymaster will use his network – "

He knew that tone of voice: it was a tease. But it was also an unwelcome idea and it was his duty to shoot it before it took wings. "Not a network exactly but we do have connections. There are still quite a lot of Turks in the South."

"And one could get you a leg of lamb?"

"He could if you'd like it."

"I'd do most things for a leg of lamb. But how is your friend going to get it in here?"

"By sea, of course – like everything else." It was a chance to tease back and he added urbanely: "You know that rather better than most."

She didn't rise to it but said instead: "Then call for me at seven o'clock. I'll give you a drink before we go. I know that you don't drink in public."

. . . Considerate as well as desirable. It was a very great prize and with patience he'd win it.

As he reached Helen Withers' villa a very much larger car was driving away. It was an open Rolls Royce and Mehmet recognised it. The two men in the back wore a sort of uniform and they had machine pistols slung on straps round their necks. There was a liveried driver and His Highness himself. Mehmet's business was to be properly curious, and curiosity was certainly justified. His Highness was king of the local castle: people called on him and were sometimes received but he seldom paid state calls in return. And this was clearly a call of formality. A motive was sufficiently obvious but that, after all, was Helen's high business. He wouldn't mention the matter unless she did first.

He was happy with this decision as he was shown in. Helen gave him the promised gin but small welcome. Something had very clearly upset her. "I've had a rotten night," she said.

"I'm sorry to hear it. What disturbed you?"

"Soldiers banging about in the garden. I went down to see what was causing the noise and they were asking

65

the servants silly questions." She gave him a look which was close to hostile. "Was that your doing?"

Mehmet was as annoyed as she was. He had intended to discuss her safety which he hadn't supposed was going to be easy. He knew that she could take umbrage easily, that the matter was going to need tact, even cunning, and some fool had muddied the waters before him. But this wasn't a matter for easy lying which in any case he wasn't good at; it was one for setting the record dead straight.

"No, it was not but I know all about it. Further, I entirely approved. What I didn't approve was breaking into your garden, pestering your servants on top of it. Those men were exceeding their orders – I'm sure of it. I'll see that it doesn't happen again."

She was mollified but not completely. "But why were those oafs at my house at all?"

"I think you know the answer to that."

"About mother, you mean? How she helped the invasion? But that was several years ago."

"Greeks haven't changed since the good God made them."

He drove her to dinner but she was still unrelaxed. He could see that something else had happened, something more serious than clumsy soldiers. He wasn't without experience, something had happened to shake her badly, and she was following established practice, taking it out on the first male she saw. There was a technique for that and he'd used it before. You didn't say: "I'm a man at your service. Out with it and the sooner the better." Instead you made polite conversation and sooner or later the woman told you.

"I heard you speaking Greek to the waiter. Knowing classical Greek I suppose that came easily."

She answered with another question. "Can you read Islamic script?"

"I can since my father had me taught it. He thought it one of the things a gentleman should know. So I can read Arabic and Persian too so long as it isn't

66

calligraphic – the sort they use as ornamentation. But unless the words are Turkish words I'm simply making noises I don't understand."

"It's much the same with demotic Greek. I could read it all right but it meant very little. I come down here quite a bit, as you know. I shop in the Greek part of town since it's nearest. The houseboy has some English but not a lot. It seemed silly not to learn to speak to them, especially since I could read already."

"How did you go about it?" Mehmet asked.

"I chummed up with the local priest who'd stayed behind. He had been taught some proper Greek at his seminary and was delighted to meet someone who knew it too. On top of that he was a first class teacher. At first he tried to convert me to Orthodoxy, but that was his duty and he soon gave it up. And I dare say the money came in handy. He wouldn't take it at first but in the end said something about his needy flock. He's a charming old boy and we get on like a house on fire. More important I've learnt quite a bit of demotic Greek."

He could see that she was relaxing slowly and decided to give the process a push. Both of them were drinking water since Nico was too good at his job to offer wine where it wouldn't be wanted and both of them hated squashes or colas. "Let's have a bottle of wine," he said. He had carefully calculated before he spoke. A sophistry might cover gin but wine was the fruit of the grape and taboo. But the Almighty was male as well as all-merciful and there'd be special rules for attractive women.

She stared at him in silent astonishment and he answered her unasked question with a smile. "The customers here are tourists or better-off Greeks. There isn't another Muslim in sight."

"Somebody might pass it on."

"That's a risk I shall have to take," he said.

"To give me what you know I'm used to?"

"I suppose you could put it like that."

"I do."

67

He had seen that he'd already surprised her and now he knew that he'd touched her too. Well, the English had strange ideas about Turks. They were excellent soldiers but inclined to be ruthless; they had a tradition of religious tolerance but step over the line into Turkish politics and promptly you got beaten to death. The English rather admired the Turks but they weren't famous for what was called sensitivity.

"What wine were you thinking of?"

"I wasn't. I've never drunk wine in my life before. I was going to leave the choice to you." He signalled to Nico and asked for the wine list. That admirable restaurateur stayed expressionless. When it came Mehmet passed it to Helen Withers.

She looked at it and then at him, trying to assess his capacity for strange drink. She had seen him drink two gins and stay unmoved and this evening he had had only one. But he'd never drunk wine in his life before . . . So nothing treacherous like an Italian Lambrusco. She looked at him again and made up her mind. He sat upright in his chair but easily; he was evidently in excellent physical shape. Like many Turks from the coastal plain many races had joined to make this handsome man. Some Venetian camp follower had left him faintly reddish hair and some marauding Bohemund blue eyes. He didn't look like a man who'd blow suddenly like a boy. She ordered them a gentle Beaujolais.

The wine came to table and Mehmet sipped it.

"What do you think?"

"It's a little early to tell." Unexpectedly he smiled, then laughed. "I know exactly what you're thinking, madam. If I do get drunk you must see me home."

"I'll put you to bed myself."

"That's kind."

"Not as kind as you are." She hesitated but brought it out. "I owe you an apology. I haven't been entertaining, I've been a bore. You see, I've had a bit of a facer."

Here it comes, Mehmet Eldem thought, and waited.

"I've been sacked from St. Mildred's. More accurately I've sacked myself. As I told you, I asked for special leave. They refused it. I must be back in ten days or I'll have broken my contract. In which case I'll be out on my ear."

"Wasn't that a little harsh?"

"It would have been if they'd liked me but they did not. I'd already dropped two resounding clangers. Care to hear? It would tell you a good deal about Oxford."

He nodded and she said: "Then here goes."

So provided she walked like a nun in Oxford her Principal would avert her eyes from anything which went on in the island. But with the senior dons she hadn't been popular. She'd been an excellent teacher with a record of academic successes but she hadn't conformed to the accepted pattern. In Oxford the classics were taught as a discipline: if you could master Latin and later Greek you could master whatever life threw against you. The system produced a reliable flow of civil servants of the administrative grade but Helen hadn't seen it like that. Rome and the ancient Greek states had been civilisations; they had been worthy of more than scholarly study; they'd been alive. And behind the accepted approach to the ancient world had been the assumption, seldom spoken but always there, that these vivid and self-confident worlds had been no more than steps to the great Conversion. Helen had dissented strongly . . . That Altar to the Unknown God and the freedman who had presumptuously revealed Him. That was a load of you knew what. Christianity had destroyed the Empire and perverted the Greeks from happy pagans, their gods half-human, warm and approachable, into the spiteful Balkan tribe you saw today. That was the way she had felt and so she had taught. It hadn't made her admired or popular. And she'd canvassed hard for the wrong man as Chancellor. In short, they'd been happy to let her go.

"So there it is," she concluded. "I'm out. I shall stay here as long as James Wedder needs me." Her tone changed slightly and Mehmet caught it. Oxford was behind them now. "Have you seen him recently?"

"I see him twice a week. He's a friend."

"And how do you think he is?"

He hesitated, choosing his words. "I think he's almost unnaturally vigorous."

"So does the doctor."

Surprised, he asked: "That odious Swiss?"

"No. I'm going to let you into a secret. I've had another doctor look at him."

"The local man won't like that."

"The local man isn't going to know. Naturally it wasn't an English doctor – English doctors can be absurdly hidebound. So I used my Dutch connections instead. I told you an uncle died of cancer so I used the doctor who saw him out. He's an old man now and no longer practising but he knows more about cancer than any clinician."

"And what did he say?"

"What I'd rather expected. A terminal of the kind James is, one who has refused dicey surgery, normally goes one of two ways. Either it's a steady decline till the time comes to go into hospital finally, or else they inexplicably perk up. They reach a sort of plateau and then crash down. Which is going to be very hard for me."

"I'm not quite sure I follow that."

"The arrangements, I mean – the material hassle. It looked as though I could have handled it sensibly. When I saw he'd reached his No Return I'd have had time to have him packed home comfortably. But as it is he may fall off his plateau tomorrow. No notice. The airport is twenty miles away and there's no direct service back to America."

"I think I could help if that happens and I will. A flight on a military plane to the mainland, then a regular scheduled flight to the States. Military doctor and nurse if necessary."

He could see that he'd moved her deeply again; she said at length. "That's extremely kind."

"Not kind – just decent. James Wedder is my personal friend and on top of that he's a friend of my country. He was stationed here when we had to come in. Several of the Powers didn't like it and one was very close to action. James Wedder kept his head and defused it." He contrived to add without sounding pompous: "We pride ourselves on paying our debts."

He poured her the last of the wine and considered. Another bottle? He decided against it. She'd drunk most of the first but he'd had two glasses. So far he might have been drinking water but it would be stupid to take an unnecessary risk. Instead he changed the subject firmly. The evening had started badly but she had mellowed into her usual good humour. He could risk a personal question now.

"What are you going to do when James goes? Another college? Or teaching in a school?"

"Another college wouldn't have me and teaching in a school is not my cup. I'm luckier than most college lecturers since in theory I don't have to work at all. Father made a good deal of money – not working as a civil servant but afterwards there were several directorships. And mother was upper bourgeoisie Dutch which means you're a very long way from poor. Or that Picasso might turn up trumps and make me rich. But all that is just theory – I've got to work. If I married and got stuck with a family I think that would take the edge off me nicely but if I don't I've got to do something active. Otherwise I'll go mad in a year."

Mehmet Eldem thought this extremely probable; he could see that she wanted to talk and encouraged her. "Have you thought of any particular line?"

"Journalism," she said. "I've done a bit." She made a small gesture of deprecation. "Travel pieces for the women's magazines, stuff about the blissful Greek islands. Either they're spoilt or utterly boring but it's easy to puff them up romantically. There may be a little more running in that but what I'd really like is a woman's column."

71

"I still take an English Sunday newspaper and when I was in England I read all three. I gathered the distinct impression that the ladies who write them are pretty competitive."

"They'd scratch each other's eyes out happily but they'd gang up against an outsider at once. But I can be pretty competitive too."

Again he believed her but it wasn't worth comment. "And will you keep your house here for holidays?"

"That's a silly question – of course I shall. I'm fond of this horrible island, tensions and all. And the scuba fishing is the best in Europe."

"I've heard the word but what does it mean?"

"It's one of those silly acronyms – Self-Contained Underwater Breathing Apparatus. No air pumped down to you through a tube. You carry your own in a tank on your back."

"Isn't it dangerous?"

"It is if you haven't been properly taught. There are various places which teach you in England but short of the Navy, which won't take civilians, I reckon the best is at Eilat in Israel. I've been trained to go down to a hundred feet. Not that you need that here in the island but I've a recognised certificate to show I could. And the boatman I use was a diver too."

"There's not much he could do if you're not on a line."

"Lines can get tangled up with harpoons."

He let it pass. "Then what do you spear?"

"Anything worth bringing home for the pot. Squid when I can get it – *calamari*. Sometimes I take a shot at an octopus." She saw his look of surprise and explained. "Oh, they're not the things you see in horror films. These aren't tropical waters and you don't get the monsters. And except by Italians they're not generally edible."

They finished their coffee and Mehmet settled the bill. Helen said: "Let's walk home – it's a lovely night. You could send a man to collect the car."

They climbed the rise from the fort and the crowded harbour. There were fishing boats and the occasional launch and a crescent moon defined their outlines. The captured gunboats were manned and lighted as usual but the practice was a simple bluff. They were incapable of serious action and in anything like bad weather they'd sink. She took his arm as they turned and began to walk home. They might have been an established couple.

Presently the houses thickened. This had once been the Turkish quarter, a ghetto. No paint on a street had divided it formally but the division had been almost tangible. Now it was less but still existed. Fear had lessened on this side, grown on the other. As they crossed the invisible divide to the Greeks a police patrol drove past them slowly. The officer saluted Mehmet, pointing to the shuttered houses. It was a gesture of reassurance rather than hate. Animals whose existence was tolerated were safely in their pens and cages. A small wind blew off the hills. It was very quiet.

Helen was holding Mehmet's arm tightly. It was the first time they had touched since a perfunctory handshake. Opportunity knocked and Mehmet took it. "I'm worried about you," he said.

"I know. You think I'm in danger and I think you exaggerate."

It would be sound technique to make a concession: a flat contradiction would get him nowhere. "I may have been once but I'm sure I'm not now."

"What's changed?"

"The danger. Up to now it's been riffraff who bought their way in through the UN post. They went for the hotels and scared off tourism. Now it's still Greeks but they're foreign-trained terrorists. They're not going for the hotels but the residents. If they can murder one or two of the prominent they reckon that the rest will run. If that happened we'd be damned near bankrupt."

"But I'm not prominent in any way."

"You happen to be your mother's daughter."

"I get a little tired of hearing that. It suggests there's

73

some sort of secret Greek *bruderbund* to avenge what mother did for you on me.''

Her grip on his arm had slightly slackened but he was committed now and couldn't withdraw; but he could make another concession and did so. "There could be something in that but it's not the real point." He drew a long breath and brought it out firmly. "Every foreigner who lives on this island knows very well what your mother did for us. Also he knows that we don't forget easily. So if we can't protect your mother's daughter they'll ask themselves who *can* we protect? They'd be frightened and with very good reason. If anything were to happen to you the impact would be a good deal greater than the murder of somebody merely prominent. And I'm not alone in thinking this."

She said at once: "So you're under pressure."

He could recognise what was intuition and had the experience not to question its wisdom. "Yes," he said, "I'm under great pressure."

"From that General?" She named him.

"How did you guess?"

"I didn't have to guess. I knew. He was a Brigadier when the troops came in and later he called on mother to thank her. After that he seems to have called pretty often. Mother wouldn't say a lot but I could tell there had been something between them. But she was alone a lot when father was working and I inherit my liking for men from her." The pressure on his arm had increased again. "I'd like to help you if I can," she said. "If you've a reasonable proposition make it."

"I was thinking of changing your servants for others. They'd be servants still and you wouldn't suffer but they'd also be efficient guards."

They walked two hundred yards in silence; finally she said: "But that *isn't* reasonable. If I got rid of them they'd simply starve. They're servants by trade and know nothing else. You're right about the hotels – they're half full. There'd be nothing in a hotel for casuals. And their circumstances are against them, too. The old man

74

potters around the garden but he's much too old for serious work. His wife is only a simple cook and she couldn't get a job as a pro. Unlike most young Greeks the boy isn't brash but the only recommendation he'd have would be mine. With things as they are that would not be enough." She repeated: "They'd starve. I simply can't do it."

He accepted this with regret but respect. "Then I'll have to think of something else."

"Please do. But it must be something I can do without shame."

They had reached the steps of her house and halted. "Will you come in for a nightcap?"

"No thank you." He didn't want another drink and what he did want he wouldn't get. Not yet.

"Then thank you for a lovely evening."

"We must do it again."

"Whenever you like."

He watched her walk up the steps and open the door. She didn't wave or even look back. Why should she? Mehmet Eldem thought. She was calling the shots and he was following.

He had begun to walk home when a man came running. For an instant an instinct said: "Danger", then faded. The man was one of his own two orderlies. He was out of breath and incoherent but his story was perfectly clear on what mattered. The British Club was burning fiercely.

They both began to run towards it. There was a glow in the sky to the east and a pall of smoke. Both decreased as the two men drew nearer.

Neither man spoke since there wasn't a need to. The wooden-built British Club would be ashes.

PART TWO

More People

The British Club had changed a good deal since its foundation in the heyday of Empire. The pleasant coastal town where it stood was by no means what had been called a hill station but there was often a breeze from the sea, it was civilised, and the beaches were a children's paradise. Officials who served a flourishing Empire sent their families there in the worst of their weather – administrators, policemen, the despised banausics who ran the local technical services. Sometimes they spent their own local leave there. The Club had been all-British and excessively rank-conscious.

That it still was but its flavour had changed. The eastern Mediterranean countries were no longer a British sphere of influence and no dusty and hard-bitten servants of Empire were available to use its services. But the retreat from the Indian Raj and its satellites had provided the club with a wholly new membership. They were men and women with a difficult decision, mostly in later middle age and mostly without an established profession outside their rank in their own Crown Service. The lawyers and the doctors, perhaps, had some hope of starting again in England but for the others the choice was stark and grim. They had their pensions and some compensation and some of them had small private means. They could return and retire to Eastbourne or Cheltenham, living very quietly indeed, far below their accustomed standard, very small beer in a country now strange to them; or they could go to this island and live quite well, still among their own kind and familiar ways.

And there'd been another influx to swell the Club's coffers. It had no background of Imperial service but its motives had been the same: a way of life. When it had considered retirement it hadn't thought of Eastbourne or Cheltenham; it had thought of Petts Wood and of dying of boredom. It had looked at the island, liked it and settled there. Quite often it was better off than the Indian Civil Servants and soldiers but it had never been entirely accepted by the men and women, now in their seventies, who had still run the Club as a private preserve. They were glad to have these people's subscriptions but had their own fours at bridge and patball lawn tennis. Perhaps rank was not as important as once but a system of caste had replaced it firmly.

Another change had been the admission of 'foreigners'. Most of the local bigwigs had joined and amongst them had been Mehmet Eldem. He had joined gladly, even eagerly. Calling on individual people you got a good idea of that person's attitudes but in a club there was a sense of community, a sort of collective opinion and outlook, and this had surprised Mehmet Eldem considerably. There wasn't a hint of unease, far less fear, but these people resented what politics were doing to them, that they'd become pawns in tiresome local games. They hadn't settled here for that. No, sir.

But apart from its use as a listening post Mehmet used the Club very little. There was a good deal of drinking though never excessive. He had never seen a man or woman drunk. But since he couldn't drink in public he'd been obliged to drink something called *nimbu pani*. It had been imported by the Anglo-Indians, a concoction of lime and sugar and water. It still bore its Hindi name and was horrible. But it was the standard soft drink of the Club and there it was. If you asked for an orange squash the waiter stared.

As Mehmet and his orderly ran the glow in the sky had almost gone but the fire brigade had brought in arc lights and as they reached the scene it was bright as day. Mehmet looked first at the smoking ruin. It hadn't meant a lot to him except as a place where a shrewd man could listen but he was glad that the squash court had not gone too. He was a man who put on weight rather easily and he had used the squash court to sweat it off. Mostly he had played the professional, a Pathan from one of the squash-playing clans. Naturally he hadn't been high on its ladder or he wouldn't have been earning pennies, but he could give Mehmet points and owe them too; and he was clever enough to keep rallies going, for Mehmet was quick on his feet and a dour retriever. He hadn't a hope of making a match of it but he could make this elegant young pederast sweat.

The fire chief came up in his oversize helmet, a survival from Edwardian England. "A professional job," he said. "We hadn't a hope. Not paraffin and not even petrol but incendiaries timed to go up together." He looked at the smoking ruins, said: "Wood."

"What happened before it went up?"

"I wasn't here but the President was. He's poking about in the wreckage now."

Maurice Fazakerly had seen Mehmet's arrival and came up to him at a steady trot. He would never see eighty again but was active. Mehmet Eldem had met many soldiers and could place them with a good deal of accuracy. Fazakerly was a type he disliked, the obscure ex-Indian army cavalryman still struggling to be thought of as smart, talking too big and too often of polo which in fact he had played on his regiment's Whalers. Normally he barked annoyingly but disaster had brought out his best; he said quietly:

"Five of them, there were – I counted. Two of the Turkish servants went for them but all they got for their pains was a beating. But they gave the rest of us time to get away. I stayed and so did that Staff Captain of yours. I wasn't armed but he had a gun. He pulled it but they shot him sitting."

"I'd like to see the body, please."

"Of course you shall. But prepare for a shock."

81

"I've seen death before."

"And so have I. But I wasn't thinking of death. Now come with me."

The body was under a sheet on the lawn where the firemen had dragged it away from the wreckage. Fazakerly pulled the sheet down and Mehmet retched. The Staff Captain was very badly burned but it wasn't the burning which made Mehmet retch. He had seen wounds and death but not mutilation.

Fazakerly put the sheet back carefully and they stood for maybe ten seconds in silence. Finally Fazakerly said:

"Nice people, aren't they, the modern terrorists? I've only seen that once before and that was on the North-West Frontier. Those bloody Pathans . . ." He left it unfinished.

Mehmet Eldem had controlled his stomach. The Staff Captain would have friends and a family . . . No, no, no, no. There were things to be done and urgent priorities. He said to Major Maurice Fazakerly:

"Tell me. How many people have seen this body?"

"The firemen who brought it out and covered it. You and your orderly. Myself and another."

"I can answer for all the Turks."

"That's good." This passed-over Major with his social pretensions was behaving with a woman's sympathy; he was asking no questions; he understood. "You may take it that I'm secure myself. The other Englishman was also a soldier." He added with an astonishing candour: "We were neither very good ones, perhaps, but we can both of us hold our tongues and we will."

"I'm greatly obliged to you, sir."

"Not at all."

Mehmet turned to his waiting orderly. He had been standing at ease, alert and watchful, but at an order came to attention smartly. He was to go to headquarters and fetch an ambulance. A military ambulance – no other. A doctor would be quite unnecessary. Also he was to deliver a message. Colonel Eldem would be calling on the Brigadier at nine o'clock. The necessary arrangements would be made between them.

The orderly doubled off on his mission and Mehmet and Major Maurice Fazakerly walked back to the knot of waiting firemen. They stood around their Chief disconsolately, blackened and dirty and out on their feet. One of them had an arm in a makeshift sling. They had the air of troops from a losing battle.

Mehmet spoke to the Chief in rapid Turkish and the Chief in turn to the men around him. All nodded – there had been instant agreement. When the Chief had finished Fazakerly went up to him. If the Chief had expected reproaches he got none. The Chief had some English and said in apology:

"I am sorry we could not save your building."

"From what I saw you had no chance." Fazakerly looked at the man with an armsling. "Shouldn't that man receive proper attention?"

"If we have your permission to leave – "

"Of course. And thank you very much for trying."

The firemen began to pack their gear and Mehmet and Fazakerly looked back at what was left of the Club. It was Mehmet's turn to show decent sympathy. "A very sorry sight," he said, "but no doubt you were fully insured in London."

"I doubt if it covers War Risks."

"The war's over."

The old man showed a flash of impatience. "Then riot or maybe civil commotion – whatever the company chooses to call it. There's always a bit in the small print to do you down. They'll wriggle and twist and somehow get out of it. And we can't afford to go to law."

"I hope that doesn't happen."

"So do I. But if it does there'll be another Club. We'll build it with our own hands if we have to." He added but without self-pity: "It was just about all we had, you see."

83

"Then a very good night to you, Major Fazakerly."

"Good night to you, Colonel, though I doubt if you'll get one."

Mehmet Eldem walked home in surprised reflection. Those Greek terrorists had got it all wrong, attributing to English expatriates the reaction of instant fear they'd have shown themselves. Burn down their Club, maybe murder a couple, and they'd pack their bags and depart in panic. Evidently they would do no such thing. Most of them were inconsiderable and some of them were quite near to poor but all of them were as tough as a soldier's boot.

*   *   *

Mehmet Eldem returned from the Brigadier, satisfied. His behaviour towards him had always been scrupulous and this morning this had paid handsome dividends. In theory Mehmet Eldem's Staff Captain had not been under the *Tuğgeneral*'s command but he'd been a soldier with a common purpose and of course he should have a full military funeral. The post mortem? There would be no post mortem. The family would be flown in to attend but by that time the body would be safely encoffined. No Turk would speak of a soldier's dishonour and if Mehmet had the solemn word of two Englishmen who had once been officers the Brigadier would accept it happily. Retreat would be cancelled and the funeral would take its place. Precious water would be used to lay the dust. They would give him a proper send-off all right and Mehmet must speak the last address. A replacement was for the General himself but good Staff Captains didn't grow on trees and in the meantime the Brigadier would lend one.

Mehmet had thanked the Brigadier warmly.

Then he should return to his office and the morning's reports. He would find one of them unusually interesting. It had come from the Brigadier's own sources and, as usual, had been copied to Mehmet.

He was reading it now and frowning heavily for Hezbollah was building up in the South. It seemed a very long time since the Chief of Police had demanded that he go on the record, had insisted that there was a greater danger than Greek terrorists who burnt and murdered; and it seemed an even longer time since Mehmet himself had thought of three-act plays. For the moment Act Two was still in progress and if these savages turned from institutions to people could easily get out of hand. Sufficient unto the day was its evil, and if it continued to run on its present lines that evil would get increasingly dangerous.

He had put the report aside for another when he was interrupted by his senior orderly who presented a card on a silver tray. The tray was Mehmet's own and he cherished it. It had been given to his great-grandfather by some Arab whose name had been long forgotten. No doubt 'given' was a useful euphemism, for the Arabs had then been a subject people and gifts were often simple extortions. Be that as it may the tray was beautiful, a fine specimen of damascene craftsmanship. Mehmet's father had presented it when Mehmet had first earned his commission and Mehmet took it with him everywhere; he regarded it as a sort of talisman. He looked at the card on the tray with surprise. It was engraved, not printed, but in florid gothic script: *Mrs Meysey du Pres* with an address in Highgate. Mehmet knew perfectly well she wasn't there. She was here on the island, His Highness's mistress. He said to the orderly:

"Ask her to wait a bit. Give her a cup of coffee while she does."

Her visit was out of the blue and he needed to think. She had been on his General's list to be called on but his call had yielded nothing of interest. He had thought her a rather commonplace woman and had been surprised that a man as rich as His Highness had chosen a woman so plainly ordinary. But he had. He had set her up in a separate house with servants and a car of her own. Whether her name was really du Pres was a secret between herself and her passport and the Meysey was at the best unfortunate. For inevitably she was referred to as Maisie. As the mistress *en titre* of the island's Great Man Mrs. Meysey du Pres had a certain standing but it was almost as anomalous as Mehmet's own. It was accepted that rich men kept mistresses but this one's choice was considered eccentric. Behind her back other women sniggered. She was – let's face it, dear – just a little bit common.

Mehmet rang for his orderly. "Show her in."

He received her standing and gave her a chair, inspecting her as she took it composedly. He put her in her early forties but she was well preserved and well made up, not extravagantly but with evident skill. Her dress was expensive and not too tight. Her servants would include a good masseuse. Mehmet Eldem had been well brought up and he always looked first at a woman's feet. This one wore shoes just a half-size too small for her. If she'd dared she would have kicked them off.

"What can I do for you, Mrs. du Pres?"

"The boot is on the other leg. I have come to give you information." Mehmet's years in England had taught him good English and given him an ear for its nuances. The accent was basically north London but also it had been worked on assiduously. Mrs. Meysey du Pres spoke exceedingly carefully.

"That's really very kind," Mehmet said. "Information is what I'm here to receive."

"I know." She took a gold cigarette case from an elaborate handbag. Her nails were not too long but a shade too red. Mehmet lit her cigarette. "Prepare yourself for a shock," she said.

"I'm prepared as far as I can be."

"Right. Then your friend Miss Withers is a spy for the Greeks."

He was used to delations, usually with some personal

86

motive, and he took it with a practised calm; he ignored the "your friend" and answered mildly. "In view of what her mother did that would be rather a change of front."

"What her mother did is now her cover."

It was the sort of illogical point he detested. Of course what her mother had done would be cover: it would be if there were anything to hide. Mehmet believed this extremely improbable and he had already decided this woman's motive. It was known that His Highness called on Helen, bringing her flowers and maybe flirting. Mehmet was not in the least surprised. Helen's wit must be an agreeable change from the rigours of this middle-class woman. Whom he'd decided was both alarmed and jealous.

But it was his duty to hear her out and he asked: "Have you anything to go on?"

"Of course. She's been seeing that Greek priest a lot, and as you know he's the head of the local Resistance."

Mehmet Eldem knew no such thing. The priest was a fine old man whom he admired. He had stayed when his superiors had run, holding his flock together in their faith. Thousands of Irish priests did the same in strange and pagan cultures across the globe. "She sees him to speak Greek," he said.

"But why? Dozens of others know some classical Greek. Why pick on a Resistance man?"

Again the assumption of guilt, the absence of fact. He would have liked to throw this woman out but she was the mistress of an unquestioned Highness. He had given up hope of any real information, deciding that he'd have to bear with her.

"There isn't a local Resistance – there can't be. Resistances are run by heroes but they do need a background from which to operate – places in which to hide and be fed. Those can only be supplied by peasants, people with safe houses and food, and there are very few Greek peasants left."

"I think that's a quibble."

"I assure you it isn't."

"Then what about burning the Club?"

"That wasn't done by a local Resistance. It was done by men who came in from outside."

"You're sure of that?"

"Indeed I am. They left their own and disgusting visiting card."

"They'd have needed a tip-off."

"Why? They came in by sea."

"Did they indeed. I find that interesting."

. . . Has this wretched woman got something after all?

"Any particular reason?"

"Yes. Miss Withers is a diver, isn't she?"

"She spears octopus."

"Octopus, is it? I thought it was squid. It doesn't matter, they're much the same." The manner had changed from malice to arrogance. "But that isn't the reason Miss Withers goes diving." She waited for she was timing the knockout.

"Yes?" Mehmet asked.

"Then here it is. Another diver comes in from the sea. That is how she passes her messages."

"Where on earth did you get that?"

"I can't tell you."

He relaxed at once: it was another fantasy. "I'll have that followed up," he said.

"And you'd better do it PDQ. The sooner that Withers is out of the island the better for your own career."

"Is that a threat?"

"You could call it a hint."

"Then thank you for coming to see me, Mrs. du Pres. Information of this sort is always valuable." He spoke with a self-evident irony but Meysey du Pres had a skin like a pachyderm.

He went with her to the door and opened it, looking at the car outside it. It wasn't her own but the Maharajah's.

He was sitting in it smoking patiently. He waved to Mehmet but didn't speak. Mrs. Meysey du Pres got in and they drove away.

His Highness was in for a boring evening.

Mehmet went back to his office thoughtfully. As Maisie had left he had shaken hands and now he washed them more carefully than usual.

Mehmet Eldem had lunched rather better than usually for he had little to do that afternoon beyond putting on his uniform in time to attend his Staff Captain's funeral. He'd had the same soldier servant for several years and could trust him to give him Excellent Turnout but he was meticulous and had checked himself. He felt he had earned a siesta in a chair.

But he had barely settled when there was another interruption. This time there was no card on the silver tray, only a simple announcement – James Wedder. Mehmet had wanted to sleep but rose. If James Wedder had troubled to call in person James Wedder had something important to say to him.

"An unexpected pleasure," Mehmet said. "Don't tell me you came in on that bus."

"No. I've hired a car."

"Then I hope you got a decent driver. Some of them are pretty dangerous."

"I drove myself."

Mehmet inspected James Wedder carefully. His manner was normal but he was working to keep it so. He was under a strain and to an experienced eye showing it. Besides, he shouldn't be driving a car at all. He was still high on his unexpected plateau but that Dutch doctor had said that when he fell off it he'd fall like a spent rocket and finally. If he did so while driving a car that would end it.

"Tell me what I can do for you."

"Tell me what really happened at the Club."

"That isn't in the papers yet. There were one or two speculations we couldn't pass."

"But it's all over the island. My housekeeper told me."

Mehmet recited the night's events, ending with a sentence of summary. "So far it's foreign-trained locals, but Greek. I'm afraid it may be something worse later but that's the state of play for the moment." He had almost said: "State of Act Two", but stopped himself.

"Whose objective will be economic. They'll be trying to drive foreign residents out and those residents bring in a lot of money."

Mehmet Eldem nodded shortly. There was no point in trying to conceal what was obvious.

"In which case they'll have a list of targets."

"So have we. And I'd guess it's much the same as theirs."

"Is Helen Withers on it?"

"Yes, of course."

James Wedder asked tautly: "Do you think she's in serious danger?"

"Yes and no. I can only tell you what I told her myself. She isn't prominent in the social sense: on the contrary she's distinctly aloof. In that sense she's hardly a target at all but in another she's a very tempting one. Every Turk on this island owes her mother his blessing and most of the expatriates know why. They'll assume that she's under our special protection and if it were shown she wasn't they'd wonder who next. They'd get frightened and leave. That's how these local Greeks will be thinking. I've good reason to believe they're wrong but it's a reasonable way of seeing it. Very Greek."

"Would you think me rude if I asked what you've done?"

"What I'd like to have done was to change her servants. I'd have put in two who'd do more than cook and clean. She turned that down flat."

"If you'd asked me first I'd have told you that. Her mother was a very Dutch Dutchwoman."

"It does her every credit, though."

90

"Credit and safety are not the same things. And so?"

"There's at least one spare room in that villa of hers. I'd like to put a man in at night."

"I doubt if she'll wear that one either."

"So do I. But I can have her covered outside the house. I'm going to put a man on her when she goes out."

"Will you tell her that?"

"What would you do?"

James Wedder considered. "I think I'd tell her. She's stubborn and proud but she's much too intelligent to be wholly unreasonable. Besides," he added blandly, "what if she is? You can always put your man on her, and provided he's only reasonably competent it's very long odds she'll never spot that you've done so."

"Then thank you very much for coming." Mehmet was getting drowsy: it was a hint.

James Wedder ignored it and went on purposefully. "I'm sorry to have spoilt your siesta but there's something else that worries me too. Helen Withers is a target personally but there are some very nice things in that house to tempt rogues. That Picasso, for instance."

"If it is a Picasso."

"If I were going to live to see my money I'd bet. Admittedly he's easy to imitate but no expert had had a shade of doubt till the old man comes along and denounces it. Give it three years or maybe five and a failing old painter's pet will be snow in the wind. The provenance was always pretty firm."

"You seem pretty sure."

"I once met her mother. She was exceedingly shrewd as well as brave." Wedder rose at last. "You've been very patient."

"I wouldn't call it that."

"I would. And you'll keep me in touch?"

"Of course I will."

Mehmet walked to the door with his guest and opened it. "Drive carefully," he said.

"Give me a single good reason why I should."

Mehmet went back to his desk and a telephone. Talk of Helen Withers' Picasso had given him a new idea. If reason wouldn't move her a good fright might. He was due to dress for a formal funeral and he earnestly wished he had had more time. More time to choose the right men and brief them, more time to arrange the details meticulously, to give the affair that Staff College polish. But he'd have to act quickly or not at all.

The night was airless, a fan was stirring, and Helen had left the window open. There was a streetlight outside and she could see the intruders, two men climbing over the sill of the window. The last two rungs of their ladder were visible. They wore masks.

She had a pistol under her pillow and reached for it. Then she checked. Even in this very unEnglish Province you couldn't just shoot men down for trespassing. If they were murderers she'd be dead by now and if they were common or garden thieves they were behaving very oddly indeed. She pretended to sleep but watched them with interest.

They went through her wardrobe and then the chest of drawers. To be expert thieves they made too much noise and from time to time they whispered together. It simply didn't fit with professionalism. A professional learnt at his mother's knee that valuables weren't kept in chests of drawers, and moreover he would have done his reconnaissance, discovering there was a wall-safe downstairs.

Presently they went away, not through the window but through the bedroom door. Helen considered following them, but though they were clearly no kind of assassin they might be armed, if only with coshes, and she was a single woman against two men. For a moment she wished she'd taken Mehmet's advice.

She lay for another five minutes, listening. They would have to take their ladder away and three or four minutes later they did so. The last two rungs disappeared from the windowsill but somehow they contrived to drop it. There was a bang and a burst of swearing. Then silence.

Helen gave them ten minutes more, then went downstairs. She didn't take the pistol with her, an action she would have thought melodramatic. She looked at the wall-safe first. Apparently it hadn't been tampered with. Then she looked around the living room carefully. It hadn't been ransacked and nothing had gone . . .

But it had. The Picasso had gone from its place on the wall.

Helen began to laugh uncontrollably. The whole business had been a put-up job and not too well put up at that.

*　　　*　　　*

The Turkish army's reputation in NATO was one of stubborn defensive courage and a disinclination to take any risks; it wasn't supposed to be good at ceremony. These opinions Mehmet Eldem knew from his time as a Military Attaché in London but his Staff Captain's funeral had belied the last of them. It had been done to almost Trooping standards, but besides the formal and flawless drill there'd been something which British soldiers might not have contrived, a sense of a collective rage that a comrade should have been coldly murdered by civilian Greeks whom this army despised. One or two others including Mehmet had more than that reason for feeling anger and he hadn't been ashamed that he'd wiped his eyes.

But this morning he was in his usual good humour as he walked to Helen Withers' villa. He was carrying a brown paper parcel. It was secured by elastic bands, not by string, for he'd been warned that string might damage the picture's frame.

Outside the house stood a waiting car, the Maharajah's open Rolls. Two armed guards sat bolt upright behind as usual but today there was no liveried chauffeur. His Highness had been pleased to drive himself.

He was coming down the steps as Mehmet arrived. This time he saw him and waved to him affably, coming round the car's bonnet to talk.

"Good morning, Colonel."

"Good morning, Your Highness." He liked to be called 'Your Highness' just once and after that plain 'you' was in order.

"I hope you're free for luncheon on Thursday. I've just been asking Miss Withers – she's coming. The Fazakerlys are coming too. I think you know him but not his wife. A little Afrikaner for some tastes perhaps, but basically a very nice woman. Myself and Mrs. du Pres of course, and a man I don't think you've met, Henry Lash. He's always been my man of business."

Sir Henry Lash was head of Hayward and Heath, the most prestigious if not quite the richest of the City of London's merchant banks.

"I'd like to very much indeed."

"That's settled then. At a quarter past twelve." His Highness opened the door of the car and got in. As he did so he glanced at Mehmet's parcel. He was much too well-mannered to show curiosity but privately he was wondering what it contained. He himself had just brought Helen flowers. He started the engine, waved again and drove away. Mehmet noticed that he drove very well.

The Greek houseboy let him in politely, ushering him into the high-ceilinged living room. Helen was sitting quietly, expressionless. "Two men in one morning," she said. "I'm flattered. And one was not in the least expected."

He could see that as it concerned His Highness the statement was almost certainly true. If the call had been a formal one she would surely have dressed to receive a personage but she was wearing a housecoat and working trousers. So far as his own call went he was much less sure. He had seen her look at his brown paper parcel but the look had been incurious, almost indifferent. And there was something in her manner he couldn't read,

94

not displeasure precisely but a certain reserve. He had other matters he wanted to talk of and he decided to keep the Picasso till last. Its place on the wall had not been filled nor had its absence been mentioned. Odd. Mehmet Eldem decided that he'd have to go carefully.

"As it happens I've had two callers myself and both of them came out of the blue. The second was James Wedder in person."

"How was he?" For the first time she was showing real interest.

"I can only say he came alone. He has hired a car and he drives himself. He arrived in one piece and he got home safely. I know because I naturally checked on it."

"That was thoughtful," Helen said.

"He's a friend."

"And I've been doing some checking too – I mean I've been ringing that doctor in Holland. He's a pretty old man but he's an honest realist. He said that if James killed himself driving that would be a happy ending but that if he merely damaged himself it would knock him off his present plateau."

"I've told you what I could do if that happens."

"You're really very kind indeed."

Her earlier reserve was fading and he accepted her next question easily. "But I don't suppose he called to talk about himself. I'd guess it was about my safety."

"It was." He held up a hand as she started to interrupt. "No, not about those Greek servants of yours. We both accept that you can't decently get rid of them. There are other possibilities, though, but if I may I'd prefer to come to them later. For my first visitor was even more unexpected. It was Mrs. Meysey du Pres, no less."

"Oh, Maisie," she said. It was toneless but communicated perfectly; it reassured him that he could tell the whole story.

"She said you were a spy for the Greeks."

"Any evidence?" Helen asked.

"None at all." Mehmet began to laugh but was impressed. Most women would have protested indignantly but this one simply asked for the evidence. "She said you were thick with the parish priest and that *he* was the head of the local Resistance."

"There isn't any local Resistance."

"I know that and I told her why."

"Anything else?"

"Just vague suspicion. She said that you had marvellous cover because of what your mother did for us."

She thought it over quietly, then said: "So if I were an agent I'd have marvellous cover. *Ergo* I am an established agent. Not a good syllogism."

Mehmet Eldem was as good as bilingual but 'syllogism' went over his head. It sounded vaguely Greek but he didn't inquire. "It's clear she hates your guts," he said.

"I know she does and for two good reasons. If you're interested I'll tell you what they are."

"Anything which goes on in this island is very much my official business."

"That sounds a little stuffy but never mind. So the first reason is her wretched painting."

"I didn't know she painted."

"Well, she does. And they're not the sort of daubs you would suppose. Not roses round the door of a cottage nor robins in the snow at Christmas. She does accomplished conversation pieces, rather in the Victorian manner. They wouldn't sell within a mile of Duke Street but she tells me they sell like hot cakes in the provinces and for once I'm inclined to believe her entirely. The shocking thing is that the woman has talent. She's a prostitute in more senses than one."

"So you panned her paintings?"

"Nothing so forthright. But she showed me one once and asked my opinion. I said, and I meant it, that our Maisie had talent, but I was thinking that if I'd had that talent I'd have used it to a better purpose. She's a woman and she read me clearly. That wasn't a good start at all."

"And the second reason?"

"Come into the kitchen – I'll show you."

They went into the kitchen together and Helen began to make morning coffee. Mehmet stared at the sink in silence. It was full of red and white carnations, the enormous forced blooms which were grown commercially. Helen looked up from the stove and said:

"The Maharajah of course, and not for the first time. That lot was flown in from Liguria where flowers under glass are a major industry."

"He told you that?"

"Of course he didn't – I happened to know. He will bring a woman four dozen carnations but he's not the sort to boast about what they cost. That would be brash and he isn't that. In point of fact he was wasting his money since I much prefer the little ones they grow here." She pointed at the sink and said: "When you grow them that big they lose all scent."

"Not for the first time, I think you said."

"I did."

"And Maisie – "

"Maisie knows and Maisie is worried."

"That His Highness might make some change in his household?" He had chosen his words with proper care.

"She's playing for higher stakes than that. She wants to be the Maharani."

He said on a reflex: "But that's impossible. Anyway, his wife is still alive."

"You know about his wife?"

"That he has one."

"I know more than that since he told me himself, and since he didn't bind me to secrecy there's no reason I shouldn't tell you too." She turned to take the milk off the ring. "They separated several years ago when he couldn't stand any more of her drinking. Now she's living in Nice on a generous allowance – he's a very generous man, you know – and every couple of months or so they dry her out. But she's a hopeless lush and can't last for ever."

"And Maisie knows this?"

"I'm sure she does."

"Very high stakes indeed," Mehmet said. He hesitated but he needed to know. "May I take it that you are not on the table?"

"You'd be very unwise indeed to do that. I'm not race conscious and he's still very male. I'd take him back to St. Mildred's and flaunt him – yes, *flaunt* him. St. Mildred's wouldn't approve at all. Not that I had married colour: if I'd married some intellectual Indian, somebody in the Commonwealth racket, that would have been all right – approvable. But to marry an ex-prince and a rich one . . ." She shook her head. "That wouldn't have been in St. Mildred's ethos."

Mehmet laughed. "Quite a scene."

"You think so?" She gave him a look which he couldn't read easily. Mostly it was one of mischief but below was a hint of feline claws. "Aren't you taking yourself a bit for granted?"

He saw he had put a foot wrong and withdrew it. "Let me help you with the coffee," he said, and began to stack a silver tray. It was solid, well made and essentially Dutch, no match for his own damascene contemporary. He carried it back to the living room and Helen poured. Presently she went to the sofa where Mehmet had left his brown paper parcel. She picked it up and began to unwrap it. "I think I can guess what's inside this parcel."

The offhandedness set him back again but he had prepared his patter and delivered it doggedly. "We've really been extremely lucky. A patrol saw two men behaving suspiciously. They chased them but they got away, presumably down to a beach and a boat. They were carrying that parcel but dropped it. I don't think it's been seriously damaged. But don't thank me too much. We've been very lucky."

"I wasn't going to thank you at all."

He was astonished but successfully hid it. Since he'd been on the island he'd been surprised more than once

98

and was getting quite good at concealing shock. He didn't comment but waited for her.

She made none but hung the Picasso carefully. When she had it to her satisfaction she went to the sideboard and said: "Half eleven. Time for an honest gin for a shameless crook."

It was early and he didn't want alcohol but her manner suggested that it might come in useful. "The whole thing stank to heaven," she said. "You were simply trying to frighten me, to soften me up to accept protection. Not a bad idea and I thank you kindly but you made an enormous mess of the whole thing."

He had recovered his poise by now and asked mildly: "How?"

To his astonishment again she laughed. "You mustn't think I'm entirely furious." This time she gave him a look he hadn't seen, not the tease look which he was getting used to but something in an older language. "In a way I'm delighted you botched it up. I couldn't live with a man who always got it right. They're more trying than the other sort who always contrive to get it wrong."

"Then how did I fall over my feet?"

"Your story to start with – it's wildly improbable. A roving patrol might have spotted two suspects but if they'd run the patrol would have shot to wound. And even if it didn't do that why should these men drop a picture weighing three pounds?"

"Conceded," Mehmet said. "And anything else?"

"A whole lot else. You told me my house was going to be guarded and any professional thief would find that out. He would hardly have used a front window for entry and he wouldn't have left a ladder outside it."

"That's logical," Mehmet said. He was playing for time.

"You're in no position to risk a sarcasm. There's more to come."

"Please go on."

"I intend to. So these men came through my bedroom window but they didn't behave like professional thieves.

99

They made a good deal of noise and woke me up. I pretended that they hadn't and watched them. The first thing they did was to search my bedroom, when any pro would have known that there was a wall-safe downstairs. And the search was absurdly amateurish. I read crime stories sometimes and they're unanimous on one thing: if you're searching a chest of drawers you start at the bottom drawer. That way you don't have to shut the others going along. These clowns began at the top and were clumsy. Further, they occasionally whispered. I have sharp hearing and the language wasn't Greek. Finally, when they went away they managed to drop their ladder with a bang." She looked at him hard but not in anger. "It was a put-up job and a pretty bad one."

As she'd been speaking he'd been assessing her mood. She was indignant rather than actively angry, and behind this was something else important. Helen Withers thought the incident funny. He could tell the truth without facing a major scene.

"I had very little time to fix it and I thought that the affair was urgent."

"What affair?"

"Frightening you," Mehmet Eldem said coolly.

She took it with an equal dispassion. "You succeeded for about ten seconds but I don't see what you were trying to do. Scare me into changing the servants?"

"I told you – we're all agreed about that. Dismissing them would not be decent. But there's another possibility and I wanted to soften you up for that."

"You may take it that you've softened me plenty, though hardly with the scare you played for. When I went downstairs and saw the picture had gone I couldn't get back to sleep for laughing. I'd laugh again if it weren't discourteous. So what's this new possibility? Tell."

"I'd like to put a man on you. When you go shopping, for instance, or visiting friends."

He had expected some protest if only formal. None

100

came. She was clearly thinking it over seriously. "So you really think I'm in danger?"

"I wouldn't have laid on that farce last night if I hadn't wanted to convince you of just that."

She thought again and then said flatly: "I realise I can't stop you anyway."

"Thank you for not making me say it. And any man sent to keep an eye on you will be properly trained and you'll be lucky to notice him. One or two others are shadowed too, though of course for very different reasons. He won't be some oaf I had to find in a hurry."

"I don't like it," she said, "but I'm also flattered. And you mustn't think I'm not grateful too."

Mehmet let out his breath in a silent sigh. The biggest fence was behind him now. "If you could give me your general movements," he said, "it would help to keep the affair unobtrusive."

"I drive out to James Wedder at least three times a week and I go shopping on perhaps two mornings. I hardly ever pay social calls. After lunch I normally take a nap and most evenings, if it's fine, I go diving. If I need the protection you think I do I shall need it down to the harbour and back again but I'm going to be perfectly safe under water."

"And neither I nor the police have a diver to follow you."

"I still think you're pushing the danger a bit but you know a whole lot more than I do. And since you're taking this trouble on my account I'll do anything I can to help. Would it make it any easier if I rang your office early each morning?"

"A great deal easier. Thank you sincerely." He was thinking that she had let him off lightly. She could be as stubborn as her mother had been and that was very stubborn indeed, but when reason was needed to solve a problem she could switch to it with apparent ease. There was something to be said for Latin and Greek. He rose to take his leave but she waved him down.

"We'll be meeting again on Thursday," she said.

"At lunch at the Maharajah's, you mean? I met him as he was leaving – he asked me then."

"It's going to be rather interesting if you've a taste for watching the worst in women. I've been there before but only to tea and Maisie was allowed to pour. That was fine with Mrs. Meysey du Pres. But if he puts me on his right for luncheon Maisie is going to simmer visibly. She isn't good at hiding her feelings."

"He said he'd asked the Fazakerlys too."

"Good. She's older than I am. That lets me out of the hot seat almost for sure."

"And somebody called Henry Lash."

"Sir Henry Lash? He manages H.H.'s affairs and his father built up *his* father's fortune."

"Then I'll call for you at twelve o'clock."

"I'd come a little earlier than that. I know you like a drink before lunch."

"Shan't I get one at the Maharajah's?"

"You will not. He doesn't drink himself as it happens but there'll be plenty of booze for infidel guests. Of whom, dear friend, you are not one. You can say a great deal against hereditary princes but normally they have exemplary manners." Her mood changed again to simple mischief. "He wouldn't wish to embarrass you; he doesn't know I've corrupted you wickedly."

As Mehmet walked home a bell rang faintly . . . "I'll be perfectly safe under water," she'd said, and that odious woman Mrs. Meysey du Pres had chattered of divers coming in from the sea. To pass messages, of all absurdities, when those Greeks could land on the coast wherever they chose. It had been nonsense of course, the purest fantasy.

The bell stopped ringing.

*   *   *

Driving to collect Helen Withers on Thursday Mehmet considered their host for luncheon. He was universally called the Maharajah but in fact he was a Muslim and

102

no such thing. He was a Mogul, and his ancestors down to the time of his father had held one of the three great fiefs of two empires. His given name was Ali Khan but he couldn't be called the Great Khan since there already was one nor, huge as his state had been, His Exalted Highness. This for the same and excellent reason. In reference books and on state occasions his father had been the Khan of Khandesh but this modest and unassuming title concealed that he ruled a state bigger than Scotland, and in the protocol-conscious world of the Princes had rated a salute of nineteen guns. Measured in terms of wealth or territory he'd been a bigger man than any Maharajah but three and one of these had ruled a desert. That tinsel world had fallen in ruins and the present Khan could hardly remember it. In any case, on this race-torn island 'Maharajah' and 'Khan' were words of an alien and incomprehensible language, distinguishable one from the other only by a handful of British expatriates. Maharajah sounded grander than Khan so that was the word which was generally used. Provided he was conceded the 'Highness' the present Khan was entirely indifferent.

He was an urbanely-mannered man of forty-nine who had left India as a boy of seven and had never returned and far less wished to. Others of his princely Order were in sour and discontented exile and some of them found it hard to live decently. But His Highness was neither discontented nor poor for his father had read the omens correctly as early as the middle Thirties and had started to build up a fortune abroad. He was in some sort of semi-feudal relationship with what was then called the Paramount Power but even if it won the coming war, which the then Khan of Khandesh had considered doubtful, it wasn't going to fight on to hold India, far less for the Princes' independence. Any sensible man must go liquid while he still could.

Moreover he'd had the means to do so. The greater part of his enormous income had come from taxes and rents which he levied at will and which in theory he could spend as he pleased, subject only to advice (which he need not take) from a British official they called the Resident. But clearly he couldn't take taxes with him. He also had four palaces but no conceivable buyer for any. But he did have one asset which could be reduced to hard cash, a collection of better than average jewellery.

He had smiled as he had discreetly sold it, for an even more powerful Prince in the South had had the same idea and miserably failed. He had called in a well-known expert from London and been told that his pretentious baubles weren't worth the sum for which he'd insured them. They looked impressive but were mostly flawed; one or two were even plain fakes. But Ali Khan's father's stones had been good ones. They hadn't been bought from local *Marwadis* nor from peripatetic Sindhi *Baibunds*, both of whom would take private pleasure in swindling a hated Muslim. They had been bought in Hatton Garden and Amsterdam, by men with an inherited eye for jewels and the knowledge that in this of all markets it paid to buy the best and accept the cost.

Much the same had applied when it came to selling. Ali Khan's father had sold into a rising market, shrewdly and patiently, never trying to sell too much at one time and never permitting an attribution to himself. By the time the winds of war had destroyed the Raj he'd been worth a million pounds in a British bank. It had been a formidable sum in the early Forties and by now had swelled into something enormous.

For Ali Khan's father, so shrewd with jewellery, had known nothing of the world of money and had put his affairs in the hands of a merchant bank. Several had been recommended but he had chosen Hayward and Heath unhesitatingly. They were as British as steak and kidney pudding, unaffected by even the faintest connection with a race which Ali Khan's father had despised. The British were going to betray the Princes but a British bank would not betray one

104

of them. There'd be no easy fixed-interest stock for an ex-Prince.

So the man they called the Maharajah thought of his father with real respect. How right he had been in more things than money! The language of his Court had been Urdu but most of his subjects spoke some sort of Hindi. He was surrounded by British Indian territory; he had no port. You only had to look at Hyderabad. Or, if you really mistrusted imperialist India, take a harder look at unhappy Kashmir. Where a Muslim majority had been ruled by a Dogra prince. And Kashmir had been seized on the rajah's say-so. The United Nations had urged a plebiscite. It had never been held and it never would be.

Yes, his father had shown great political judgement and had left his son a wealthy man. Not oil-baron rich perhaps, but still a Croesus by any ordinary standard. When his father had died he had come to the island; liked it; bought a house and settled. That had been in the day of Greek rule, so he had bought a villa from a mainland Greek merchant and later added to it to meet his needs.

In this establishment he now lived in considerable style. No clinging to the periphery of what was absurdly called the jet set, trading on a now meaningless title, no decline into a genteel poverty when India had reneged on its promise to pay the ex-Princes decent allowances.

But though he lived in some state it was not ostentatious. He could barely remember his life in India and in any case was far too anglicised to regard ostentation as other than vulgar. He was the biggest man on the island, respected, and if few men knew his real wealth that suited him. For he had money in America, in Great Britain, West Germany and Japan. None in France. His father had mistrusted the French since an ancestor had hired them to fight the Mahrattas and they'd run away at the first shot fired.

The Maharajah permitted a secret smile. He even had property here on the island for his money had financed

105

the new mine and he still held most of the company's equity.

Only he, the General and the Man knew this, and of course Sir Henry Lash of Hayward and Heath. That sort of knowledge could be as dangerous as the Black Death.

Helen Withers had kept her word and had telephoned to Mehmet's office that she meant to go down to the sea that evening. He found her checking her diving gear and watched her with a real satisfaction. He knew nothing of aqualungs but could recognise a competent craftsman. She hadn't been boasting when she'd told him she'd been carefully trained. It was his experience that the real enthusiast seldom resented friendly questions and he broke a comfortable silence to ask:

"What does that bit do?" He pointed at the inflation vest.

"That's what brings you up again when you've had enough. Pull this cord and it fills with air and up you pop."

"You learn that in your training?"

"Of course. And for the first few dives there's always an instructor with you."

"What happens if you have a blackout?"

"You won't do that if you've been properly taught. You've got to keep the pressure in your lungs the same as that outside you in the sea. That's basic."

"Suppose you get a heart attack."

"Before any reputable school will accept you they put you through a pretty stiff medical. If you've any sort of dicky heart you simply won't get taken on."

He persisted but she wasn't offended. She could see that he was concerned for her safety and respected a man who wanted to know the facts. "Suppose some sudden incident – "

"Such as what?"

"A shark coming at you."

"There are no sharks in these waters – they're too cold below the immediate surface. But if I saw a shark I'd

106

inflate at once. I'd come up as though the devil were after me." She pointed at the cord again, "I've dived enough now to make that a reflex."

"And you're diving this evening. I thought you didn't go swimming after a heavy meal."

"Not immediately after – no. But we'll be out of the Maharajah's by three and when you bring me back here I'll sleep for a couple of hours. I shan't be in the water before six. That's plenty of time to digest a meal."

"Even a heavy one?"

"The one thing you won't get at His Highness's is the standard English curry lunch. Curry, he told me once, was a giveaway. Hindus thought it up to disguise stringy chicken and goat. The more doubtful the meat the stronger the curry."

"Heresy to an Indian, that."

"Ali Khan is insistent that he isn't an Indian. He tells me that every time he calls, which is now a steady once a week." She gave him again that look of pure mischief. "Not that you have cause for worry but Maisie is worried sick unto death. I wonder how she'll behave to me at lunch. It's a litotes to say that she isn't a lady."

"Litotes?"

"Sorry. Greek. Understatement." She had finished with the aqualung and began on the underwater harpoon.

"An ugly-looking weapon," Mehmet said.

"What I go for are pretty ugly animals. As I told you I only kill the adults."

"Does it work on some kind of spring?"

"Compressed air."

"Would it kill a man?"

She considered this carefully. "If he were fully dressed it probably wouldn't but if he were wearing a wetsuit it might." She took off her apron. "It's time to go."

The Maharajah received them in the long verandah which ran the length of the villa behind it. The façade had been in debased Palladian but it hadn't been as debased

107

as all that and the Maharajah, who'd had an eye for line, had decided that to put wings on each end would be a blatant architectural solecism. But more rooms he must have for his servants and bodyguard and he had solved his problem with taste and judgement. Two new wings there now were but they weren't in extension; they ran backwards towards the sea and the beaches, enclosing the formal garden a Mogul loved. There were few flowers but clipped hedges of oleander, the death flower of the Hindus whom his father had ruled, and a stone basin in the centre with a fountain which sometimes worked and sometimes did not. Today it was in good heart and order.

And Helen had been right about the drink: there was plenty of that for those who wanted it, served by servants in a modest livery, but His Highness himself was drinking tomato juice. Like Mehmet he wasn't distressingly pious, his faith rode him on the lightest of reins, but he saw it as a matter of manners. For instance, there was champagne this morning but it hadn't been offered in glasses on a tray. Its existence had been discreetly mentioned but anyone who preferred gin or sherry was welcome to choose what he normally drank. Similarly with drinking himself. To break a fundamental rule before people who would know you were breaking it would be an action in very poor taste indeed, and to offer drink to a fellow Muslim would be to offer a wholly unwarranted insult. So Mehmet, too, was drinking tomato juice.

At one end of the verandah was an easel with an unframed painting and presently His Highness waved at it. "Mrs. Du Pres' latest," he said.

They were clearly expected to show an interest and they gathered round the picture to admire. It was something which Maisie had so far not tried, not a vicarage lawn with a decorous croquet party but apparently a sale of bloodstock. Three horses were being held by grooms and a group of potential buyers was quizzing them. In the background was a man on a rostrum, presumably the auctioneer. It was as glossy as a society magazine.

The Fazakerlys both said: "Charming" and meant it, for it was a painting which would find a good home, if not in the Fazakerlys' own then in another with very similar tastes. Mehmet Eldem thought the horses looked wooden but managed a word of conventional praise. Helen hovered on the fringe uneasily, conscious that Maisie was watching her closely, knowing that she knew her opinion, hoping she wouldn't be asked directly. Finally it was Sir Henry's turn. In age he was Fazakerly's contemporary but in every other way his opposite. He spoke softly and had formal manners; he was elegant and tall and thin. His enemies, and in his life he had made many, accused him of a worldly cynicism. The cynicism he would have gently rebuffed but he would have admitted to a healthy realism. High-minded persons would not have found him congenial.

And he was distinguished by more than a striking appearance for it was known that he took an interest in painting. In fact he collected Mogul miniatures, bare-breasted beauties done with great delicacy, a mile from the contemporary copies which were painted by the dozen in Delhi and sold to unsuspecting tourists.

He advanced to the head of the group and changed spectacles, staring for what seemed an inordinate time while the others held their breath respectfully. In point of fact the picture made him wince. He was thinking as Helen Withers had thought: so evident a minor talent and so evidently a total falsity. He was too old to feel obliged to lie but in eighty-two years had learnt diplomacy. He stepped back from the painting and bowed to Maisie.

"Sincerest congratulations, madam. That piece should sell extremely well."

The Maharajah led them all in to luncheon.

He had solved any tiresome question of protocol by seating them at a small round table. He had signalled to Mrs. Fazakerly to sit on his right and to Helen, the next senior guest, to go to his left. Beyond that they had seated themselves at their pleasure, Fazakerly next to Helen, then Mehmet, with Maisie and Sir Henry Lash to close the circle. Maisie was watching Helen closely and His Highness was watching Maisie closer. He was as urbane as ever but not entirely relaxed.

Conversation was at first rather stilted since two current topics were taboo by unspoken consent. The burning of the British Club had provided good talking for several days, casual gossip unknowing the incident's horror, but one could hardly bring that subject up in front of the club's grieving President and a Colonel of the Turkish army who had lost a Staff Captain by brutal murder. The other subject nobody mentioned was the future of the whole community. These people wouldn't be frightened out but they realised they were in serious danger. Mainland Turkey must really step in and take full control.

But this again could hardly be said in the presence of a Turkish official.

Presently the slight chill thawed. Mrs. Fazakerly drank champagne very seldom and it had mellowed her Afrikaner bark and growl. She had spent her married life in India, in cantonments in the torrid plains, very different, she was insisting stoutly, from life in the overpraised *Jewel in the Crown*. The Maharajah up to the age of seven had lived in yet another world and he was listening with a genuine interest. The British had betrayed his Order but they had also been amazingly hardy. On the other side of the Maharajah Helen hardly needed to speak at all. Fazakerly had never been talkative and Sir Henry was engaging Maisie. Mehmet had time to watch the small drama.

Sir Henry was being polite to Maisie but he thought that she was tiresomely commonplace and when he saw that her mind was elsewhere was grateful. He attended to his food with interest which at the moment was a partridge with saffron rice. The rice was served separately and as he liked it, *al dente*. He wondered if the tale was true, that in the old days even the minor rajahs kept a special cook to cook their rice. There wasn't the barest hint of curry and the vegetable was aubergine, perfectly done. The wine, he thought, was a solid Mâcon. He was eating his lunch with the respect it deserved.

Maisie was only pecking at hers, declining Mehmet's gambits with clichés, her interest on the Maharajah and Helen. Helen was in fact almost silent since Mrs Fazakerly was going strongly and His Highness was feeling stretched to engage her; and to her left the lady's husband said little. Helen wasn't stealing the party and she'd hardly exchanged a word with His Highness. It was Mehmet's impression that Maisie was relaxing.

She wouldn't have been if she could read her master's mind. He had decided to marry Helen and dump herself.

Of the two the former would be much the more difficult: Helen wasn't the sort of fruit which fell from the tree. You had to go extremely carefully and so far he had been doing just that; he had been making advances but playing it long. On the first occasion he had taken her flowers they had been a tribute to a visitor of wit and beauty. On the second he had mentioned his wife. She had just been dried out for the fourth or fifth time but always she had gone back to the bottle and her very expensive doctors had warned him that unless she made a real effort of will her expectation of life was not enormous. Helen had shown a decent sympathy. No more.

On the third occasion he had gone a step further, mentioning his wife again but adding that when she died he'd be alone . . . But hadn't he any family? Yes, he had two sons in England. One had a job in Hayward and Heath and the other was a successful architect. Both were British citizens and both were married with growing families.

So there it stood for the moment, interestingly. He was confident that she'd read his message, much less confident of how she'd received it. For his part he desired her ardently and he knew she wasn't indifferent to men. But what did he have to offer *her*? He had wealth

111

and a great position still but he didn't think Helen would marry for these; he was virile and active, fair-skinned, rather handsome, but Helen could take her pick of men to her bed. His best chance was that she wanted to settle down. Women who had lived full lives often did, and he knew that she had lost her job. As for Ali Khan as a mate she knew that he'd been a considerate husband; he'd been considerate with a wife who'd offended him, then, when he'd known it was hopeless, he hadn't divorced his children's mother but had set her up in Nice in suitable state.

Yes, his best hope was that this experienced woman would be tempted by the bait of marriage. He must play his cards accordingly, slowly.

Maisie had never been mentioned between them because no mention had in any way been necessary. Helen Withers knew more than enough of the world to know that a mistress was always expendable, and that was what the Maharajah would do. He would buy her a house in some suitable ambience, not somewhere frequented by other artists who would see through her at once and reject her, but in the sort of place where any painter increased the community's sense of self-esteem. And of course there'd be a generous settlement.

Ali Khan had been thinking this but with one doubt. Maisie might not be dumped so easily. He knew that she meant to trap him when she could. She might make terrible scenes and worse. She had a little money and her paintings sold. She might even refuse to leave the island.

In which case, the Maharajah thought grimly, Mrs. Meysey du Pres would meet with an accident. Her vulgarities had begun to annoy him and he wasn't a Mogul for nothing.

He wasn't to know he'd have no need to take action.

The outside guests had gone their ways and Maisie had gone upstairs to rest. She never said 'to sleep' or 'siesta' since both implied a Latin slothfulness which she vaguely felt was unbecoming. On the other hand

112

an English lady was entitled to rest on a hot afternoon.

The Maharajah and Sir Henry Lash had gone back to the verandah to talk. There was a table with more coffee and brandy and a servant hovered behind it discreetly. Sir Henry declined another brandy but accepted a second cup of coffee. Ali Khan asked him: "Anything else? A cigar perhaps?" and when he shook his head dismissed the servant. He was a considerate man and therefore well served.

They settled in comfortable chairs to talk business, for although they had met earlier that morning no decision had been reached on the issue and Sir Henry had come to the island to get one. He finished his coffee and said decisively:

"I think you ought to sell that mine at once."

"Do you mind if we run through it again?"

It was annoying but Sir Henry wasn't surprised. When they had chatted earlier he had realized that the Maharajah had had his mind on something else. Normally he was sharp and attentive with an appetite for business and money so it must be something out of the ordinary. Sir Henry had wondered what but at luncheon had seen. He was no longer young but was still sharply observant and had noticed that Mrs. Meysey du Pres was watching Miss Withers closely. He had never met Helen Withers before but she was a striking and clearly intelligent woman. Sir Henry knew quite a lot about Maisie – more, in fact, than His Highness knew. She had been many things but never intelligent and at the moment had begun to fade.

Sir Henry emitted a tiny sigh. It was half of regret and half satisfaction. There were many things against growing old but there was one and quite unquestioned advantage. It released you from any desire for women.

So Sir Henry, though annoyed, was patient. "Let's start at the basic position, then. That mine's lease is held by a British company which is registered at the office of Hayward and Heath. It is worked by Turkish engineers

113

and guarded by regular Turkish troops. The directors apart from myself are dummies. They hold the few shares which the law requires of them but ninety-seven per cent of the equity is held by the Khan of Khandesh, yourself. Not in his name but in that of a nominee. That nominee is another of my companies. All this was done to protect your interest. We both of us know what that mine produces."

"I thought we never talked about that."

Sir Henry laughed. "So it's mixed pyrites. But all of it is shipped to Israel and Israel has no known use for pyrites. If it had it could buy them cheaper elsewhere. And Israel has powerful and ruthless enemies."

"If you're thinking of that attack on the mine – "

"I was not. That was done by comparative amateurs, by refugee PLOs as it happened. But in the seething pot of Arab politics the PLO no longer rates highly; it has been overtaken by much more dangerous men with a powerful state behind them, backing them; and it's known that these men have established a foothold in the South of this otherwise charming island."

"You fear another attack on the mine?"

"I doubt if that's on. I fear for you."

The Maharajah was puzzled and openly showed it. "But I thought you said you had hidden my interest."

"You can't stop intelligent men making guesses."

"Pretty big guesses."

"But are they so big? Consider the economics, please. This Province is extremely poor; it lives on tourism which has been severely damaged, and the mine, or rather the huge lease we pay on it, is now its principal asset by far." Sir Henry leant forward. *"Where did the capital come from to start it*? You're the only really rich man in the Province."

"The company – " the Maharajah began.

"A company formed in the last few years to mine and sell a commodity of which there is an enormous world glut. Who, in the ordinary way, would put up money for that?"

114

"You think the finger points at me?"

"I didn't say quite that. But I think it might."

"Give me a moment to think." His Highness fell silent, finally said: "Let's get this straight. Anybody who troubles to do so can find out that the ore goes to Israel, and Israel doesn't buy what it doesn't need. That will seem curious to Israel's enemies and on top of that they'll have excellent Intelligence. They will know about the recent extensions to that establishment down in the dark Negev. They could put two and two together and get it right. Israel's bitterest enemies are building up in the South of this island. Yet you said another attack on the mine wasn't on."

"There are more ways of disabling that mine than by storming in and blowing it up."

"For instance?"

"By changing its effective ownership. Presumably into Arab hands."

"Only I could do that."

"Precisely my point."

The Maharajah was quick and asked only one question. "Suppose you got my written order to transfer my holding to somebody else?"

"In the ordinary way we'd honour it unquestioningly. But if we knew or suspected you were under duress we would certainly think very hard before doing so."

"Suppose you started getting parcels containing, say, an ear or even a leg?"

"The Israelis once said of Golda Meir that if she were kidnapped and chopped into pieces they still wouldn't yield to Arab extortion."

"You're not an Israeli."

"No, I am not. I'm a civilised man with a horror of torture and that puts me at a disadvantage if I had to deal with an Arab extortioner. Also I'm a merchant banker so there's only one thing I could do and I'd hate it. I'd have to take it to the Foreign Office and I doubt if that would help you a whit. They'd think of their own position first. May I speak to you as your father's friend?"

115

"Mine too I hope."

"It's a very great honour. So not only do I think you should sell but I know of a willing, an eager buyer. The Baron von Ems wants that mine rather badly. Mining is one of his major interests and I could negotiate a very fair price. He has a villa here and is coming at any time."

"But if you've worked it out that I may be in danger the Baron may have worked out the same. Why should he buy that danger with the mine?"

"Because in his case it's hardly a danger at all. Security in the FGR is a great deal tighter than anything here."

"I'm allowed my own bodyguard. They're ex-soldiers and they're adequately armed."

"But trained against professional terrorists?"

"I take your point and I'll think it over. But I like it here – it suits me perfectly. I like the Turks and the Turks respect me. Whatever I may be now or have been I'm a genuine, copper-bottomed Khan. That's a headstart in a Muslim country. I get on very well with the Man. When my wife dies I hope to re-marry and settle here. I won't be bullied by Arab scum."

"But you'll listen to Baron von Ems?"

"I will listen."

"In that case," Sir Henry Lash said quietly, "in that case I shall take a siesta."

Mehmet Eldem dropped Helen at her villa to sleep. She had been silent on the journey, preoccupied, and he knew her well enough by now to know that she would resent social chatter. But as she got down from the car she said:

"I hope you enjoyed your lunch."

"Very much."

"I told you you wouldn't get curry."

"You were right. What I really got was a sight of a way of life."

"A way of life," she said reflectively. "Yes, I suppose you could call it that."

116

There was a question he wanted to ask her badly but although they shared a clear understanding to ask it directly would be close to impertinence. On the other hand they had their own private shorthand.

"That sort of life – would it ever attract you?"

She read the message and looked at him straightly. "If I could have it on my own terms it just might."

"Then I wish you good fishing."

"I hope I get it. If I catch enough cuttle for two I'll give you a ring. Come to luncheon tomorrow and eat *calamari*."

"Thank you. I'd like to."

In the event he was to see her sooner and it wasn't to discuss her food.

*   *   *

Helen had set her alarm for five o'clock but woke without it a few minutes before. She dressed leisurely and carried her aqualung to the car. The houseboy would have done it for her but she was fastidious to the point of fussiness in letting no one but herself lay hands on it. She put it carefully on the back seat and drove to the harbour.

She was conscious of a rising excitement for her hobby's hold was increasing with every dive. These weren't great waters for scuba enthusiasts – not the sort they showed on television, where shoals of gorgeously coloured fish swam lazily past reefs of coral to background music of overstrung violins and tinkling bells. This sea was reasonably warm but not tropical. There was no coral and surprisingly few fish, even fewer to tempt the diver who dived to hunt them. There was the occasional shoal of red mullet and little else edible.

But Helen didn't dive to kill fish; she dived for the excitement, the challenge, the reward of a world forbidden by natural law. It changed with every mood of the sea, often hostile, occasionally almost welcoming. It was addictive as the hardest drug and, if you took

117

foolish chances, every little bit as dangerous. She often dived without a gun but she'd promised Mehmet *calamari* and if she saw a cephalopod the boatman was always grateful for the gift. Very few people cared to eat them since even if boiled for days they were tough, but Spiro seemed to have a market.

He met her on the quay with a smile, a mainland Greek who might have been any age. He had a cap of grey hair, baggy breeches and bare legs. These were the colour of ancient mahogany. He'd been a diver in the Royal Greek Navy, but that had been in the days of helmets, of air pumped down from the surface through a tube. He regarded all aqualungs with an undying suspicion but realised that his client understood hers. He saw the harpoon and smiled again.

"I hope you get one, lady."

"I hope so too." Helen knew that he'd be glad to have it. Once he had made a prosperous living with a queue of tourists anxious to hire him but the tourists had diminished notably when the hotels had become a target for hoodlums and now Helen was almost his only regular. She had heard him curse the Greeks of the South. He was a mainlander and thought little of them.

He started the engine and they slipped out of the harbour. Its waters were filthy and you had to go out at least a mile before finding the sort of sea you wanted. Helen went into the cabin to change.

When she came out the boatman had glasses up, staring at a ship ahead of them. He gave the glasses to Helen silently. He seemed uneasy and she wondered why.

"What is it, Spiro?"

"That ship – she's a warship, a coastal patrol boat. And she isn't one of ours."

"How do you know?"

"They're both in the harbour."

"Can you see her flag?"

"She isn't flying one."

It was certainly a little unusual but Helen felt none of the old man's disquiet and no reason to postpone her dive. The ship was stationary, broadside on to Spiro's, and she had noticed that its gun wasn't manned. She had harnessed her backpack while still in the cabin and now she put on flippers and slung her harpoon. Last of all went the mask and the meticulous final check. Then she sat on the gunwale and dropped in backwards.

As the water in her wetsuit warmed Helen realised she'd been dropped on this spot before. The seabed was mostly shale or mud but here there was an unexplained patch of sand. It was surrounded by rocks like an undersea arena, and in those rocks she would find her prey.

But for the moment she wasn't thinking of fishing but rapt in the physical pleasure of diving. Conditions were exceptionally good. The sea here was shallow, five fathoms at most, she would guess, to its bed, but at the moment she was swimming above it. She had a torch which she'd need when she went down to the rocks but at her present depth she could see without it. She was alone in an alien world, but its mistress, and she abandoned herself to its mysterious bliss.

When this faded she remembered her duty. She had promised Mehmet squid for luncheon and swam down to the rocks where there were sometimes several. Today she saw none but she did see an octopus. It was half hidden in a fold in the rock but her light reflected back from its dull eyes. It looked a little too big to be decently edible but Spiro was always grateful for anything.

She had unslung her harpoon when some instinct woke sharply. She turned and saw another diver. He was coming towards her fast and he held a knife. A second of incredulity, then the reflex of overwhelming fear. Helen raised her harpoon and fired and the glass of the diver's mask disintegrated. There was a rush of air upwards and for a second he stayed still. Then he started to writhe helplessly, a salmon on a merciless gaff. She

119

could see his face in contorted terror, then he sank to the seabed and lay there unmoving.

Helen went up to the surface fast. That too was a reflex, not conscious action. She was more frightened than she had ever been.

Spiro had been watching the coastal patrol boat but she hadn't moved and he was feeling less anxious. He had been watching, too, for Helen to surface and when he saw her do so he waved. The procedure when she came up had been agreed: if she surfaced any distance from him he would take the boat to where she trod water but if she were quite close she would swim to it. Today it was barely twenty yards but Helen was showing no sign of swimming. He waved again but she didn't wave back. Perhaps she was tired though he'd never known her so.

Not seriously worried yet he began to move the boat towards her and almost at once had to fight down near-panic. His sharp old eyes could see her face and behind the mask she was as white as a shroud. Her eyes were moving, she seemed to be breathing, but she was clearly in very serious trouble. He manoeuvred the boat till it almost touched her, put a knife in his belt and slipped over the side to her. He had many times seen her remove her mask so he knew how it fitted and took it off. She managed a half-smile.

"Help me, please." It was almost inaudible.

He felt a moment of sardonic amusement. This woman was severely shocked, very possibly she had injuries too, but an English lady would never forget to add 'Please' to an imperative tense.

He had dropped anchor and the boat hadn't drifted but he was faced with the considerable problem of getting Helen up and into it. But there was one thing he could do and he did it. He drew his knife and cut the harness of the aqualung, watching it sink with satisfaction.

. . . Damned, newfangled, dangerous things they were.

120

That decreased his problem but didn't solve it. He was a wiry old man but not a powerful one: to get into the boat himself and then try to pull her in wasn't on. She was quite a big woman, still wearing a wet suit, and they were too far out to tow her ashore even if he'd been sure she'd survive it. It was the rope ladder or they were both of them dead.

It had never even occurred to him to leave her while he went for help. He was a seaman with the code of his trade.

"Can you manage the ladder?"

She didn't answer. She had spoken when he'd taken the mask off but now she was semi-conscious, in shock.

He put her hands round the ropes which held the ladder's rungs but he didn't believe she had strength in her arms to pull. Then he dived and took her flippers off, putting one foot on the lowest rung. Perhaps some instinct, some muscular memory . . . Then he moved behind her, still in the water, trying to get some leverage from below.

It was agonising, exhausting work. Sometimes she made a rung or two, but then she would slip and he'd have to start again. Finally, with his strength almost gone, he had her up breasthigh to the gunwale. With luck he could just about manage it now.

"For Christ's sake hold on."

He scrambled into the boat himself, careful not to rock it more than he need. Helen hadn't fallen back but he could see that she was swaying dangerously. He put his forearms under her armpits; he prayed. For a moment he felt defeat; she didn't move. Then suddenly, like a reluctant cork, she came. They were both of them on their backs in the cabin cruiser's well.

He took a minute to get his breath, then rose. He knew what he must do and quickly: he must get her out of that wetsuit at once. If he didn't she'd chill into hypothermia – pneumonia at the very least. But it would be polite to inquire before he stripped her.

"Can you get that wetsuit off?"

121

He thought she shook her head very slightly but in any case had no time for the niceties. He felt for the waterproof zips and pulled them. Then he went to the cabin for blankets and covered her.

He turned the boat towards the shore and made for it. He seldom opened the throttle fully but now he did.

In the harbour he made fast quickly and went ashore. A man was sitting on a bollard, smoking, and Spiro walked across to him fast. "There's been an accident," he said. "Come at once." The man was another mainland Greek and on the island they were a closeknit community. Each knew the other's business perfectly and this man, Spiro knew, was a plainclothes policeman, one who had stayed behind and served the Turks. That didn't in the least offend him. He had stayed himself and been treated decently.

The man on the bollard addressed Spiro respectfully. He was the boatman's very distant cousin and Spiro was very much older than he was.

"What can I do for you, cousin?"

"Come quickly."

"An accident, you said? To whom?"

"To your charge." Normally he wouldn't have said it but in his community very little was secret and he knew that a senior plainclothes policeman would not have been sent to the harbour for nothing.

The policeman didn't protest. "Let's run."

"To run will attract attention."

"You are right." They began to walk briskly. Spiro said as they went:

"Your charge is in my cockpit, stark naked. I had to get her wetsuit off. Naturally she is under blankets."

"A case for a doctor?"

"I do not know. From your point of view you should pray that she isn't."

"I've been taught a little first aid."

"Then apply it."

The boat was moored with her cockpit away from

122

the shore. They clambered over the cabin roof and the policeman pulled Helen's blankets down. "No external wound," he said. He felt Helen's limbs and then her stomach. "No limbs broken and stomach is palpable."

"What do we do now?"

"Keep our heads. Is there a bunk in your cabin?"

"Yes."

"Then we'll take her down there and try to keep her warm. Have you any more blankets?"

The old man nodded.

"Then we'll use everything you've got."

Between them they carried Helen below. Spiro said: "I've got some brandy."

"The worst thing possible. Have you any milk?"

"A little powder in a tin."

"Then mix some and warm it." The policeman pointed at a portable stove. "If she comes round try to get her to drink it. I'm going ashore to ring my master. If we're lucky we'll get her away without scandal." Unexpectedly the policeman bowed formally. "Cousin," he said, "I am proud to be so."

The Brigadier had been cooperative again and by the time the policeman, with Mehmet Eldem, had returned to Spiro's boat in the harbour a military ambulance had already arrived. A doctor was in the cabin with Helen and the other two men went down to join him. He had made his first examination. "No physical damage," he said, "but heavy shock." He looked at Mehmet Eldem and added: "I gathered from the Brigadier that you wanted this matter handled discreetly so let's get her back to her home at once. There's no medical risk in moving her and my guess is that she'll recover fast. I'll get the attendant to bring a stretcher."

They carried her out to the waiting ambulance. One or two passers-by stared curiously but no crowd collected and no one asked questions. The doctor was in uniform and that was enough to secure respect.

His forecast that she would recover fast was right. In

the ambulance she opened her eyes and when she saw Mehmet held out her hand to him. The doctor said:

"No questions yet. I'll make another check when we get her home. Let her sleep for a couple of hours if she wants to."

The doctor made his check and departed. "I've given her a very mild sedative, just enough to make sure that she sleeps for a bit. Apart from the shock she's remarkably healthy and when she wakes up she'll be almost normal."

Helen woke within the two hours predicted, looking round the familiar room. "I'm sorry to have been a nuisance."

Like the boatman Mehmet was sharply amused. The English were an extraordinary people. "How do you feel?" he asked.

"I feel a fool. Passing out like a Victorian flapper."

"Care to tell me what happened?"

She told the story in a matter-of-fact way and at the end he asked a single question. "What will happen to that frogman's body?"

"It will stay on the bottom unless somebody goes for it. If I'd wounded him he might have had time to inflate and come up. But I didn't wound the man – I drowned him. I saw his face behind the broken mask . . ." She rolled over in bed and made a promise to the listening wall. "And that's the last time I'll speak of that. If I dream of it I'll go to a shrink." She rolled back and swung her feet to the floor. They had put her into a short cotton nightdress. "Now I'm going to get up and have some food."

"You could have it in bed."

"I loathe eating in bed."

It was imperious and he watched her carefully. Her spirit was clearly whole but her body was not. She put weight on her feet and rose in one movement. Then she staggered but didn't fall. He had caught her.

"For God's sake be careful." Instinctively he had spoken in Turkish.

It didn't matter since she was swearing heartily, not

124

at Mehmet Eldem but at herself. When she'd had some relief from the swearing she said:

"Silly, weak women. They make me sick."

"I'm delighted you're not a man."

"I know. And I'm delighted you are one. Now help me dress."

He said a little doubtfully: "Shouldn't I send for the housekeeper?"

"No." She flared again. "Goddammit, Mehmet, I'm not a prude. I've just been stripped naked by an old Greek boatman."

"That's rather the point."

"What is?"

"He was old."

It wasn't spoken in jest but it made her laugh and he could see that the laughter was excellent medicine. She had almost completely relaxed and said:

"So stop behaving like a shocked little boy. I'll tell you where everything is. Just bring them one by one and give me a hand."

"I'm going to sleep very badly tonight."

"For what it's worth to you, so am I." Her next remark changed the subject brutally but he had learnt to read her apparent inconsequences. "Have you been seeing a lot of James Wedder?"

"I go out to him whenever I can."

"So do I. While he lasts."

*   *   *

Inwardly the Man was furious but like most pragmatists he was also fair-minded. Helen Withers held a very special position and she'd been attacked from the sea by a murderous frogman. That attack had disgraced all four men at the table but he wasn't a clairvoyant himself and he didn't expect his servants to be so. Recriminations would be entirely futile.

"All we can do is to limit the damage. The Club was burnt down and we couldn't hide that. Have we a chance of hiding this one?"

125

Mehmet Eldem said: "I think we have. I've asked Miss Withers to say nothing about it. She agreed."

"It was a promise freely given?"

"It was."

"Then I think we can accept it confidently. She has always been well-disposed to us and I cannot see what she'd gain by talking. What about the boatman, though?"

"He doesn't know."

"But surely – "

"All he knows is that a diver surfaced in distress. Scuba diving is not without risks, even for an experienced diver. Aqualungs have been known to fail or the operator can make a mistake."

The Man took time to think this over but finally he nodded acceptance. "Then the position overall is this. These men may be only Greeks but they're formidable and we know that Hezbollah, the really hard terrorists, have been building up their strength in the South. Do you think that the two have made an alliance?" He had turned to Mehmet Eldem again. "You know more of the great world than I do. If I may say so without offence that's why you're here. Do you think Hezbollah has taken over those Greeks?"

"No, sir. Their objectives are too different for that. The Greeks are trying to drive out our residents but Hezbollah will want to neutralise the mine. That would damage our economy too but that won't be the Hezbollah's motive. Theirs is simpler but internationally more dangerous. The ore from our mine goes in bulk to Israel and Israel is Hezbollah's first enemy."

"Thank you, Colonel. Very clear. Very lucid. So for the moment we're back on these Greek irregulars." The Man looked in turn at the Brigadier. "Is there anything you can do with soldiers?"

The Brigadier had expected this question and had painstakingly prepared his answer. "If this were a conventional war the conventional wisdom would call for a preemptive strike. These men live in a sort of camp.

126

It isn't a big one and it's a concentrated target." The voice took on a faint hint of bombast. "I could bomb the whole thing into dust in ten minutes. Alternatively I've a parachute troop and the aircraft to put them over the target. But neither operation is possible. My terms of engagement do not permit it."

"Nor do mine," the Man said and left it at that. He thought the Brigadier's speech a waste of time since everyone at the table knew that the last thing he wanted was to attract world attention. That limited him to defensive action but he had long ago accepted that. He turned resignedly to the Chief of Police. "Then what is the police position, please?"

"Not good. The ex-soldiers who settled here and were glad to join the police have dried up. The locals take far longer to train and I shan't get another draft for a month."

"So we're under-policed for another four weeks."

"I'm afraid that's how it stands inescapably."

The Man fell into reflective silence. When he spoke it was to ask peremptorily: "Where's that ship which carried the frogman gone?"

"She has retreated outside our territorial waters and in any case we have nothing to challenge her. Just two old CPBs which break down."

"So she could land men at pleasure? On any dark night. Equally she could take them off."

"I'm afraid that's a fact."

"Very well." The Man had made up his mind and said: "So all we can do is to try to outguess them." He swung in his chair to Mehmet Eldem again. "Who are the most probable targets?"

"So far they've burnt down the British Club and gone for a woman they'll know we're in honour bound to protect. The next obvious targets are prominent persons, which means in plain language the richest residents. These are Baron von Ems and the Maharajah."

"The Baron von Ems is not on the island."

"But his house is being prepared to receive him."

127

"And the Maharajah is allowed his own bodyguard."
The Brigadier said: "For what it's worth."

"I understand you perfectly, Brigadier. But there is
nothing we can do about that. His Highness is both proud
and stubborn; he comes from a long line of Princes; he
would never accept that his person be guarded by men
who were not his personal servants."

"Leaving him Number One target."

"I fear so. So all we can do is to watch and pray and
I don't think it's impious to stress the watching." The
Man rose in decision. "Good morning, gentlemen."

The others had risen too to take their leave when the
telephone on the desk rang sharply. The Man picked
it up and his grim face froze. "We were wrong about
the Maharajah. What has happened is that they've murdered his woman. Please sit down again while we get the
details."

Maisie had been doing her shopping. She preferred to
do it all in one shop and the only one anything like a
superstore was well into what was still the Greek quarter. She was attended by two of His Highness's guards.
For this sort of occasion they didn't wear uniform nor
carry the automatic weapons which they did when they
rode in their master's car. And the Brigadier had been
perfectly right: they had handguns but were far from
expert.

One had been standing outside the store and another
had gone inside with Maisie. The street outside was
noisy and crowded but the guard had noticed nothing
suspicious.

An inconspicuous passer-by shot him dead. He hadn't
even drawn his weapon.

A second attacker joined the first and they went to
the shop. The door was open and they threw a grenade
in. There was an explosion and instant panic. They went
inside.

The scene would have sickened a normal man but
these two were very far from normal. The second guard

128

had been caught by a splinter and was lying on the floor in a heap. Maisie was one of the few left standing, holding on to her trolley for support. They shot her twice in the back and walked outside.

In the street they joined the thickening crowd. They were Island Greeks with the local accent and had nothing in the world to fear provided they didn't behave suspiciously. Such as running from the scene of the outrage. So they melted into the chattering crowd. A single policeman had arrived on a bicycle and they even asked him a silly question. He told them sharply to move on.

It was the excuse they wanted and they walked to the beach. But not too fast. They had been landed the previous night by launch and the plan had been for the launch to return when they radioed the CPB. But it would take it half an hour to reach them and that half an hour would be anxious waiting.

But whatever Manichee god loved terror had sent them an uncovenanted bonus. The beach had a jetty used mainly by fishermen and an elderly one was starting his engine. They had been trained to love killing and shot him down.

Then they motored away to the waiting CPB. On the way they threw the fisherman into the sea.

The four men had waited, shifting uneasily, till the story was before them, complete. The Brigadier said:

"Excellent planning. Two sorties from one trip by that ship."

The Man controlled a sharp flick of annoyance. The military mind moved down tramlines of its own. It would appreciate a good plan at once but it wouldn't be till somewhat later that the sheer political horror bit.

The Man himself was already gripped by it. This was a crisis and he was responsible. He said slowly and with an unusual formality: "We cannot afford another such incident. If there is one we must admit defeat. And only mainland Turkey can help us." He looked at Mehmet

129

Eldem speculatively. "Colonel, you are here to advise. Pray do so and pray take your time."

Mehmet was glad of a moment to think for he had to get this right for the record. When he had his thoughts in order he said:

"As I understand my country's policy it is very much the same as your own – lie low. There are plenty of Turkish politicians who think we shouldn't have stopped where we did; we should have taken back the whole of what was once ours. There are others who think we were right to stop but that we should federate this Province to Turkey. Both views may well have been right in their time but now we are bound by the terms of the Ceasefire. Anything which broke those terms, anything which looked like breaking them, would be a very grave political risk. There would be loud Greek protest which no doubt we could ride but there's another and much more powerful state which wouldn't be pleased if we lit another fuse."

"Nevertheless I am going to ask for help."

The Brigadier said: "I don't want more troops."

"Your views on using troops as police are well known." It was delivered as a snub and the Brigadier frowned.

"But I'd give my hope of heaven for more men." It was the Chief of Police who was speaking now. "Policemen, coastguards – call them anything. But men to seal the coast at all costs. Men on the beaches, men on patrol."

"Which is exactly what I intend to ask for." The Man held up his hand as all three started talking. "But there are established techniques of successful diplomacy. Everyone but an American learns them at his mother's knee. I cannot go to Turkey myself."

The Brigadier, who'd been piqued, said curtly: "Why not?"

Though it hadn't been his intention to do so the Brigadier had been stretching the Man's long patience. Now it snapped. "I must beg you to try to think politically. It is possible for me to leave the Province but impossible to conceal that I'd done so. Equally where I had gone – to Turkey. The Greeks would make great play with

130

that; they would say that we were in serious trouble and for once what a Greek was saying would be the truth. The Prime Minister would no doubt receive me but he wouldn't concede me civilian police."

"You were thinking of *military* police? Several hundred?"

"Gendarmerie. What else is there if we're not to fall apart as a state?" The Man turned to the simmering Brigadier. "But I wasn't thinking of sending you. You could go to your *Tümgeneral* and he to the next man up the military line. He in turn would go to the Chiefs of Staff. By the time the proposal reached those who rule it would be just another importunate demand."

"Just as you please," the Brigadier said.

"I must ask you not to interrupt." The Man went on with his cool exegesis. "On the other hand Colonel Eldem has lines to the top. He was appointed by the General himself and has authority to go to him direct."

"I would never have used it without asking you first, sir."

"It isn't a question of asking *me*. I'm asking *you*."

"If you put it like that – "

"You've an outside chance of success. No more. I realise that. But nobody else has a chance at all."

Mehmet Eldem said uncertainly: "I can hardly refuse."

"How long will it take you to make your arrangements?"

"If it's urgent – "

"It's urgent."

"I could pack in an hour."

"A car will call for you in sixty minutes. A plane will be at the airport to fly you out." The Man rose and held his hand out simply. "I thank you," he said. "I thank you sincerely."

In the aircraft Mehmet was thinking uneasily, wondering if he'd been set up for a fall and whether when he got to Turkey he wouldn't be quietly retired or maybe worse. He had had one success, the assault on the mine, exactly the sort of affair he'd been sent to smother, but after that three failures handrunning. He couldn't fairly be blamed for a burnt-down Club and though Maisie herself was unimportant her protector very certainly wasn't. But it was the attempt on Helen which seriously worried him. For the General would have heard of this and the General had known Lady Withers well. That was putting it at the very lowest and even though the attack had failed it was hardly a feather in Mehmet's cap. He could well be in for a cool reception.

And behind any personal fears was Hezbollah, a looming menace increasing inexorably. It had been mentioned that morning but not pursued, and the news of Maisie's murder had pushed it aside. That hadn't decreased its power for evil.

And in the South of the island its grip was tightening. Originally they had been admitted as political refugees by a government which had blinded itself to the lessons of Lebanon and had been anxious to cock a political snook at the West which it believed had betrayed it. These men had not been put into camps – for one thing the original trickle had been too small – but farmed out to unsuspecting Greek families, their board and lodging paid by the government. That hadn't lasted for long as the South had been warned. Quite soon other men had appeared with arms and they were terrorising their unhappy hosts. They weren't living now in friendly homes but had seized one side of a square, four houses. Now there was no pretence of refugee status; these men had their organisation's admitted aims. They had connections deep into Syria and Iran – some people said well north of those. Their objective was a state within a state, a firm base from which to pursue their mischief.

And they were uncomfortably close to complete success. The South had come to its senses too late, offering them money to leave. This had been declined contemptuously. Then it had refused further entries, a policy which had had no effect. The coast of the South was as open as the North's and men were coming in almost nightly. The reports took a gloomy view and with reason. Things were not as bad as in Lebanon, the writ of the government still ran generally, but there were pockets of Hezbollah power where it did not. The situation was reported as critical for the classical symptoms were there for analysis, the extortions from the small businessmen, the kidnapping of two much bigger. It was believed that one had paid a million and a million bought food and further arms. The Greeks of the South had left it too late and the price of annoying the West was being paid. Hezbollah, the Party of God, was in business.

Mehmet twisted in his uncomfortable seat. The PLO had been the openers who had rung up the curtain with a typical, hopeless attack on the mine. Then had come the Arab-trained Greeks who had burnt down the Club and committed an obscenity. That act of his three-act play was still on stage and Mehmet was on his way to his General to ask for help in getting it off it. But if that succeeded there would still be Act Three, Hezbollah with different aims and ethos, with money, connections and far better training. He couldn't foretell what they'd do and didn't try.

Perhaps he shouldn't have taken this job at all. He'd been the opposite of the traditional harlot. She had had power without responsibility but he'd had the latter without the power. Or rather without it unless he went to the top.

Which now he was doing but not by choice.

Only one aspect gave him mild comfort: the dread word 'liaison' had never been spoken. Liaison officers were of two well-defined types: there was the junior officer whom his regiment didn't wish to take to war and was accordingly offered to General Duties; and the man who had had command and failed. Neither was at all well considered; both were lambs for sacrificial slaughter. But the General had never once said 'liaison'; he had been honest and called the appointment anomalous.

Mehmet sighed softly. He would very soon know the worst. He would indeed.

The aircraft slipped up to the ramp to Reception and another full colonel came forward to meet him. He was in uniform and that was ominous.

. . . I'm going to be put under open arrest.

But the Colonel saluted and said politely: "Your appointment with the General has had to be postponed, I'm afraid. There have been developments which we hadn't expected – international developments. You're to hold yourself in readiness at your hotel. Have you brought a uniform?"

"No."

"Then I should go to your regiment and borrow one quickly. You're going to meet some important people – some very important people indeed."

PART THREE

Top People

The Lash family was international, for the original Hanseatic stock had spread. It had dropped a single consonant from its name and flourished mightily. Lashes were merchants or merchant bankers in Great Britain and the United States, in Canada and in Argentina. Mr. Secretary Lash was an American citizen and his family had been so for six generations. He hadn't wanted the job of Secretary of State, serving a President he considered a peasant, but service was in his blood by now as firmly as in his British cousins'. One of whom, Sir Henry Lash, was coming to see him later that morning. It would be the only pleasant break in a grinding day. For he had to dissuade his parvenu President from taking some half-baked action in the Near East.

(Why did he have to call it the Middle East when the eastern Mediterranean basin was so clearly the beginning of Asia?)

The Near East was Elliot Lash's nightmare, as pathless as a primeval rainforest, but of the animals which lurked in it two were the most outstandingly dangerous. He wrote it down to clear his mind.

Greece and Turkey have been at loggerheads for centuries and still are.

No Arab, wherever he sits in the spectrum, is other than bitterly hostile to Israel.

These are separate problems but meet in that island's mine.

Elliot Lash read this through and tore it up. It was a very long way from being original but if he stuck to it he'd avoid tempting by-paths. He decided he'd think of Greece and Turkey first.

That situation was reasonably stable. Greece was a third class power at best but was behaving as though she possessed real muscle, closing waterways between pairs of islands which had been open to all shipping for decades; she was even making futile noises about an area which was unquestionably Turkish. But she couldn't risk a war with Turkey. She had a frontier with that state in Europe and the best of her army faced Turkey across it. But both sides of it were heavily fortified and any war there would be stubborn and bloody. Besides, Greece had indefensible outposts. At the first shot fired the southern Dodecanese would go. Cos and Rhodes were within range of Greek aircraft, but their Effective Time Over Target would be measured in minutes, whereas Turkey, from much closer bases, could saturate the airspace over them. They were garrisoned but not by good troops and Turkey was known to have modern landing craft. The vaunted Greek navy? Simply irrelevant. No admiral, particularly a Greek, would dare send his ships where carrier-borne aircraft would be taking on those based on land. Greece was becoming a noisy nuisance but she wasn't going to start a Near Eastern war.

But Israel and the Arab nation (a pretentious phrase but he hadn't invented it) might do so and all too easily could. They had already fought three bitter wars and in one of them only American aid had saved Israel from a sharp defeat. And short of war there was the problem of terrorism. There were as many organisations active as there were quarrels between the Arab states. It was a minefield but one that had been recently swept.

For in its original form the PLO was dead, its swaggering leader no longer credible, his paymaster looking for other clients more effective in the business of terror. The bulk of the Palestinian refugees were herded in camps in northern Lebanon, menaced by an Arab militia which Syria would like to disarm but dare not. There were pockets of armed men here and there who still owed allegiance to their discredited leader and from time to

138

time the Israelis bombed them. But the movement as a whole had splintered, the fighting men melting away into new groups which held more promise of success by war. And the number of these alarmed Mr. Secretary.

He took a paper from his high-security safe. The procedure to do so took nearly a minute but when he had it he read it with falling spirits. The most dangerous group had of course been Fatah and this had been ejected from Syria, which was anxious to mend its bridges with the West. But its leader was still active and formidable and below him was the order of battle of what was generally called the Rejectionist Front. There was the PFLP, the Popular Front for the Liberation of Palestine, the Abu Musa Group and Fatah-Intifida, all with a record of murder and massacre. Arabs were notoriously fissiparous and this ragged-tailed rabble of quarrelling factions might quietly have been ridden but for one thing. All of them looked far east of Palestine, deep into the Middle East proper, deep into renascent Islam. Above all there was Hezbollah, the Party of God, and a powerful state inspired and armed it.

Hezbollah was building up in that island, the island whence Israel imported pyrites.

Elliot Lash had started to think of the mine when he was interrupted by a smooth young official (why did Foreign Offices all over the world attract that particular type?).

"Good morning, Mr. Secretary. The President would like to see you."

"I have an appointment with him at five o'clock."

Amongst the President's official advisers Mr. Elliot Lash was the odd man out. He deplored the shift of power from east coast to west, into hands which he considered incompetent. He would serve since his country demanded that duty but he wasn't Mr. President's lackey; he would see him at five o'clock as arranged. The President might lose his uncertain temper but Mr. Secretary Lash would be coolly indifferent.

139

Milton and Harvard had given him that. But if he turned really nasty and fired him then Elliot Lash would accept that happily. He had once been a Senator and could be so again, for he was very well thought of in his native New England.

The official said: "I was to tell you that it was very urgent."

Urgent indeed! Lash almost laughed but caught it in time. He had been urgently summoned before and had wasted his time. The President would have been listening to one of his cronies, some All-American Colonel-boy or an ex-sailor with a taste for intrigue. That had happened before, the result a disaster. Elliot Lash said with a freezing formality:

"Please convey to Mr. President that I will do myself the honour of attending him at the hour which he himself arranged."

When the official had gone Lash returned to serious, anxious thought. Hezbollah was building up in that island, and its mine . . .

He was one of very few who knew the truth. Others might have guessed it. He *knew*.

Most mixed pyrites held vestigial traces of something which was much more valuable but vestigial was the word that mattered. These traces were commercially negligible, not worth working in a normal economy. But then Israel wasn't a normal economy. There was much about Israel he didn't like but he didn't withhold his admiration. What an extraordinary race the Jews were! Now there was that new complex deep in the secret Negev, built at crippling cost and quite uneconomic, but wringing from the island's ore what Israel most needed to survive.

Lash didn't believe the current scare that Israel had a stockpile of nuclears which it intended to use to destroy the Arab world: on the contrary he gave them the benefit of a generous doubt. When they insisted they had no nuclear weapons they were probably telling the literal truth. The literal truth but by no means the whole of it, for nobody with good Intelligence believed that they couldn't produce one in days or hours. If the Arabs for once could act together, a contingency which Elliot Lash thought improbable, if they pushed the Israelis with their backs to the sea, then Arab capitals would go up in a final dust.

That balance of terror suited America well. The Arab states would have guessed what he knew. There wouldn't be a fourth Arab–Israeli war.

But no, that was superficial at best. Hezbollah was not an Arab state but – he sought for a word and found it – a disease . . . The two provinces of what had been Jordan which Israel had in practice incorporated? To Hezbollah they were only marginally interesting. Their first objective was the destruction of Israel and that wouldn't suit Lash's country at all. It was the ultimate guarantor of Israel and the Jewish lobby was the most powerful of all. And, and, and . . .

And the mine from which Israel drew her new strength was situated in that turbulent island. Where Hezbollah was building up men and arms. On the face of it that didn't make sense. The original PLO refugees had made one hopeless attack and been promptly humiliated. Hezbollah was better armed and trained, more strongly motivated, wholly fanatical. But they would hardly make the same mistake, they would hesitate to fight regular troops head on. So they must have some other and better plan and Elliot Lash couldn't even guess it.

Sir Henry Lash was shown in with some ceremony. The two men had met before at parties, in Washington and New York, and at meetings, but they had never before met one to one.

"Good morning, Mr. Secretary. Good morning, cousin."

"Good morning, Sir Henry. Good morning, cousin."

It would have taken a genealogist to have stated the relationship accurately, the Firsts and Seconds and innumerable Removals, but the Lashes were a

141

closeknit clan and Elliot Lash of a recognised sept of it.

"Will you take a glass of sherry?"

"Thank you." Mr. Secretary's own drink before luncheon was gin but he knew that his kinsman never drank it. "Fino or amontillado?"

"The amontillado, please."

"I drink that myself." It was a lie but Elliot Lash had *hidalgo* manners. He poured and Sir Henry sipped.

"Excellent."

"I'm glad." Lash looked at his distant cousin appreciatively for he greatly admired this elegant Englishman. He knew that he wouldn't see eighty again but his mind was as good as ever. Sir Henry said courteously:

"It is kind of you to receive me like this, especially as I've come to pick your brains."

"If I have any left in this miserable job. And no doubt you will offer a fair return."

Sir Henry laughed. "I will do what I can. So I've just come back from that combustible island. When is it going to blow its lid?"

"I wish I knew but truthfully I don't."

"I ask because I've a customer there."

"I know – the Maharajah. Your father was his father's man too, and between you you made him extremely rich."

"He has money everywhere, including the island."

"I shouldn't have thought there was much to invest in."

"There is just one thing. I must leave it at that but you will know what I mean."

Though he didn't like sherry Elliot Lash drank some; he did so to earn time to think. When he hadn't been a Senator he'd been working in the family bank. He said finally, very quietly indeed:

"I imagine there is a British company and an enormous holding held by nominees."

"You'll know I can neither confirm nor deny it."

"Quite so. You are a banker and I was once. But I'm entitled to say and say I do that if I were the beneficial owner I'd be out of that island by the first plane available."

"It's as hot as that?"

"I'm afraid it is."

"Cousin, I am extremely grateful."

"Then let's go to luncheon. This town is full of pretentious restaurants which ape the cooking of other countries but I belong to a little luncheon club which does American home cooking well."

Elliot enviously watched Sir Henry eat. He ate enormously with a hungry child's gusto but his stomach was still as flat as a boy's. Elliot had to watch the calories, especially the carbohydrates. They ate and chatted and parted with a mutual respect . . . When next coming to London Elliot must inform Sir Henry first. He wouldn't be able to offer him food like this but one of his clubs had an outstanding cold table and another a rather interesting wine list.

They went their separate ways, Sir Henry to sleep. The luncheon had been long and leisurely and at eighty Sir Henry felt no shame in an afternoon nap. He would do it properly, take off his clothes and go to bed, and a mysterious internal clock would wake him at six o'clock precisely. When he would take a shower and change his linen. He was a fastidious old man as well as an elegant.

But before he dropped off he counted two regrets, for he would have liked to tell his cousin more. Without formally breaking a customer's confidence he had conveyed to a fellow banker obliquely that that customer held an unusual investment and the fellow banker, now a senior statesman, had given him the advice he had wanted. That had been in his customer's interest and Sir Henry had felt no hint of scruple. But there had been two other matters he couldn't mention, or not without risking a breach of trust. The first was that there was a willing

143

buyer for an investment which might be endangering its owner, a German industrialist called the Baron von Ems; and the second he had learned as His Highness's friend. For he was fearful that the Maharajah would turn down any offer the Baron made. He'd had luncheon at His Highness's house and he was as observant as a seagull wheeling for food. He knew that his host's wife was sick, and an extremely attractive woman had also been a guest. The mistress *en titre* had been nervous and edgy. There might be something in that or there might not, but there was another and more concrete matter which Sir Henry knew because the Maharajah had told him. He had asked his advice as an older man whose father his own had wholly trusted.

For the Man who ruled this uneasy Province had discreetly approached its most eminent resident and asked him to accept its Presidency.

Sir Henry had asked for a day to think, then answered that the proposal was workable, at any rate from the Man's point of view. His policy was to let time wash over him – *quieta non movere*, Sir Henry had thought – and they were busily writing a new constitution which of course would be democratic in form. In practice it would make little difference, the Man would continue to hold the reins, but it might help to soften world opinion and as such would be in line with policy. And it would be clever to appoint as President a man who was neither Turk nor Greek. Crowns had been peddled around before, the crown of Greece a quite recent example. The Victorian princes had been too grand or perhaps they had simply been too well-advised to tangle with unreliable Hellenes. In the end, Sir Henry rather thought, they had settled for some Danish nonentity.

All this was past history but currently relevant. For if Ali Khan had been seriously tempted he would hardly sell his stake in the island and he certainly wouldn't be able to leave it.

Sir Henry Lash rolled over in his bed. He was Ali Khan's friend but he wasn't his guardian.

He slept.

Mr. Secretary Elliot Lash did not. He would have liked to drop off in his chair but dare not. Somebody might come in and see him and the ethos of the American people did not permit that officials take afternoon naps. Instead he dealt with a tray of papers, then settled to think of his meeting at five o'clock.

He did so with increasing depression since his President was clearly nervous and when he was that his reactions were predictable: first he'd propose a preemptive strike and when he had been talked out of that he'd despatch Elliot Lash to shoot the trouble.

And Elliot Lash detested travel. He had a comfortable house which was now too big for him since his wife was dead and his children off his hands. Several eligible ladies had signalled strongly that they were willing to be the second Mrs. Lash, but his sons were married and had given him grandchildren, his daughter had a child on the way. He was a tidy-minded man who hated fuss, two experienced live-in servants looked after him, and it had seemed to Mr. Elliot Lash that a second woman, not greatly desired, was as likely as not to upset his domestic machine.

He returned to Mr. President, frowning. He would probably ask him to pack his bags again and Elliot Lash resented doing so. Moreover there were Assistant Secretaries more than adequate for the ordinary mission. Was there trouble in some third class country, Paraguay, for instance, or maybe France? Then one of these men should surely go. He had long since demoted France from the top league. She was an unreliable ally and he saw no good reason to pack his bags for her. In any real trouble she would go her own way.

A coloured telephone on the desk rang unexpectedly.

145

It was seldom used since the President preferred interviews. Lash picked it up, waiting till the scrambler's hum faded. An exasperated voice said shortly:

"I've been trying to raise you most of the afternoon."

"I'm afraid I had an engagement outside. In any case we were meeting at five." It was polite but not cordial.

"Please come over at once."

"May I know what's happened?"

"Okay." (Mr. Elliot Lash would have said: "Very well") "There's been big trouble in that miserable island. I've had an urgent signal – "

Lash asked sharply: "From whom?"

The President told him.

. . . So it wasn't from one of his amateur armies, it was from an established and highly reputable Agency which Elliot Lash entirely trusted.

"I'll be over at once."

He put the telephone down to evade a discourtesy: the President liked the last word, a sharp one; then he sent for his car and got into it thoughtfully.

He was going to have to pack after all.

*　　　*　　　*

Several thousand miles to the east of Washington two men were talking in a dingy room. Occasionally there was firing outside as one militia sniped at another but neither paid it the least attention. Both were outside and beyond mere civil war; they were the High Command of the Party of God with boundless ambitions and a complete dedication to an Islam which had been bloodily born again. The senior had had many names but at the moment was simply known as Daoud. The second man was his Chief of Staff. Daoud was asking a simple question.

"How many men do we have on the island?"

The Chief of Staff said: "About a hundred. More than enough for something concentrated. We're not interested in bankrupting the Province, only in neutralising that mine which feeds Israel."

146

"By snatching the Maharajah's person and persuading him to part with it to us."

The Chief of Staff considered carefully. "With anything like luck that can be done."

"We won't go over the plan in detail but it's our duty to eliminate luck. More accurately to eliminate the chance that somebody else acts first and bitches us."

"You were thinking of the PLO? They still have a handful of men on the island."

"I was not. The PLO can safely be left to wither on the tree. Their motives are quite different from ours. I was thinking of those murderous Greeks. They won't have thought of a kidnap – they've no reason to make one – but His Highness would be the most tempting target to kill. And a dead Maharajah would abort our own plan."

"I hadn't thought of that."

"Then think of it. I gather they live in a sort of camp."

"They do since their paymasters find that convenient. It is unfortified and security is low."

"I would like them removed from the present equation."

"That can easily be done."

"Then at once." Daoud had started to rise but the Chief of Staff checked him.

"And after we have His Highness's person? You spoke of persuasion but it is sometimes resisted. He comes of a martial race, you know."

Daoud's dedicated, ascetic face split in one of its rare and worldly smiles. "It's the saints who sometimes resist persuasion. Ordinary brave men do not. Or not for long."

The local Greeks had had arms and some training but had been no sort of match for the men of Hezbollah. Who were much better disciplined over much longer periods and were all of them politically dedicated. The camp was wired but the wire was symbolic, and Daoud's Chief of Staff had been right. There was no obvious need for tight security and in fact it was no better than casual.

A single man had been patrolling the perimeter and a sniper ended his listless stroll with a single shot. An RP grenade smashed the guardhouse to matchwood and the wooden gates were blown by a limpet.

Hezbollah went in in five separate groups. One man was enough for the cookhouse and messroom where nobody was expected nor found, and another took the hut which was used by day. The other three groups were of five men each and they ran to the three dormitories fast, tight knots of disciplined, well-rehearsed men. The explosions had woken the sleeping mercenaries but they didn't sleep with their arms and were therefore helpless. More grenades tore the hesitant men to pieces, then the raiders went in with their automatics, systematically making sure that no man lived.

The seventeen men re-formed outside and marched to the gaping gates in the wire. They didn't run now – there was no need to do so. The latrines were on the left as they neared the gates. The leader gave a sudden sharp order and bursts of automatic fire raked them.

The Party of God reached its trucks and drove away. The operation had taken four minutes precisely and there hadn't been even the hint of a casualty.

*   *   *

The President handed the message to Elliot Lash. He checked its provenance first, that it wasn't from some half-baked amateur, then settled in a chair to read it. Mr. President had sat down too and Lash gave him an appraising glance. He was anxious to air his own opinions but in his time at the top had learnt just enough manners to let Elliot Lash read the message first. He did so and said:

"So it's the Brownshirts getting snuffed out by the Blacks."

148

Mr. President looked completely blank. In the merciless in-fighting of American politics he was a professional of the highest class but he knew little of European affairs and in his heart he despised European history. Lash saw that he had made a mistake and said smoothly:

"I was thinking of a recent precedent for the really hard men killing off the merely tough."

But Mr. President wasn't interested in precedents. "How hard are these Hezbollah?"

"Very."

"Then why did the South let them in in the first place?"

"I don't know." It was literally true though, knowing Greeks, there were guesses. Besides, Elliot Lash had an established technique. He let Mr. President ask the questions he wanted to, answering them as shortly as possible, by monosyllables if those would serve, and then, when he'd exhausted the obvious, coming in himself with a practical suggestion. If, he now thought grimly, he had one.

"How many of them are there by now?"

"I can only say they've been coming in steadily. Clandestinely. By sea. By night."

"So if they're powerful enough to wipe out those mercenaries they could be powerful enough for something bigger."

"You have only to look at Lebanon."

"Jesus." The President was now visibly rattled. "But surely there are Greek troops in the South."

"Whose numbers and, more important, whose arms are limited by the terms of the Ceasefire."

"We can't have Hezbollah taking over the South."

"No."

"Turkey would intervene to protect the North."

"Yes."

The President said: "You can have my airplane." It was a considerable concession. He loved his personal aeroplane more than his wife.

149

"Thank you, but I really think not. It would only attract the attention I wish to avoid."

"When can you leave?"

"Tomorrow morning."

"For the island directly?"

"I don't propose to go near the island." The President looked blank again and Lash explained. "Both the North and the South are client states. Greece supports the South, Turkey the North. Those countries are where real policy is made."

"So you'll go to Athens first?"

"Certainly not. The Greeks are in more than their usual muddle, and muddle or not they'd try to drag us in; they'd see this affair as something they could exploit. No, I shall go straight to Ankara where I have good connections and even a friend."

"Turks can be difficult too."

"I know. But at least they don't have delusions of grandeur. On top of that they owe us a favour. We looked the other way when they took the North."

The President said: "Good luck."

"I shall need it."

When Elliot Lash went on one of his travels he liked to keep his entourage small. A predecessor had been tiresomely flamboyant and had earned himself the nickname of Ringmaster but Lash had found that the fewer he took the more likely he was to achieve some success. Nevertheless there was an irreducible minimum. It would be foolish to travel without an expert, the man across whose desk the detail came, and since he might not be impressively senior the protocol of Lash's Department demanded that the senior come too. This Elliot Lash thought a waste of money but it would be foolish to antagonise civil servants upon whose goodwill a Secretary depended. Convention also demanded two others. The first was a bodyguard whom Lash thought unnecessary, for if a serious attempt were made on his life a single man would hardly forfend it;

150

and the second was an official translator. Again Lash thought him expensively otiose. He was going to see the General himself and the General had more than adequate English. If some term cropped up which needed translation it was unlikely to be translated misleadingly.

So apart from the expert who might occasionally prompt him there was only one other man Lash thought necessary. This was his elderly personal servant who had been with him for twenty years, in his days as a banker and now as Mr. Secretary of State. Elliot Lash wouldn't move without him. He was an ageing rural Black, very close to the earth, and endowed with an indefeasible good sense. Lash was not ashamed to consult him. In any choice between imperfect courses (and any political choice was one between evils) he was as likely to pick the less damaging as any committee of Ivy League pundits.

The six men sat in the First Class silently, each of them with a separate worry. Elliot Lash's would have surprised the others for he was worrying about the climate in Ankara. He could stand a good deal of heat and even mildly enjoyed it but like the Man in his island he disliked air-conditioning. When his wife had died he had had it torn out, replacing it with old-fashioned ceiling fans. Except, of course, in the servants' quarters. They were mostly Black and superstitious, and to serve a madman offended the Lord. They would have packed their possessions and left next day.

But he woke in very fair form next morning. His room had been air-conditioned as he'd feared and he hadn't been able to open the windows, but he'd been tired and had managed seven hours sleep. His servant had brought him his own brand of coffee and the rest of the early morning's ritual, which so often seemed to foretell the day's events, had gone well. His shave had been both smooth and successful. (He used a cut-throat.) He never ate food on aircraft, never, and his regular bowels had opened normally.

151

He went to the General's office alone, knowing that if it should come to hard bargaining the experts would have to be called in to chaffer, and three men rose to greet him as he went in. The General he already knew, who introduced the other two gracefully. "I don't think you've met the new Foreign Secretary, and the Colonel is Colonel Mehmet Eldem. I've asked him to be present this morning because he knows more about that island than anyone else. You could call him my personal eyes and ears there."

And other things, Mehmet Eldem thought. Such as whipping boy if the lid blows off.

They all sat down.

The General said without preamble: "We all know what Hezbollah's just done. We're here because of what they may do next." He turned to Mehmet Eldem. "How strong are they?"

"According to our last information about a hundred well-armed men. And increasing all the time as others slip in."

"Who have refused all demands to leave the island?"

"They know they can only be ejected by force."

The Foreign Secretary said: "Yet ejected they must somehow be. Lest much worse befall and perhaps quite quickly."

"Militarily we could do it ourselves but politically that's out of the question. It might just be on if the situation got desperate but by that time it would be far too late for a quick and decisive in-and-outer. We should find ourselves at open war."

They're playing it very cleverly, Lash thought, feeding me the basic position by dialogue which they've no doubt rehearsed. And they know the ground rules too. If it came to an unavoidable choice between Turkey as an ally and Greece, my country would have to come down for Turkey. Turkey, like France, is simply *there*, geographically an essential ally, but unlike France she would certainly fight. She couldn't defeat a major offensive but anything short of that she could delay.

Whereas Greece is outflanked in the Med already and in any case wouldn't fire a shot.

And the other basic ground rule goes like this: the United States will do anything possible to avoid a war between NATO allies.

. . . I wonder what they're going to ask me to do. Turn a blind eye to that quick in-and-outer? Perhaps use the veto in the Security Council?

The Foreign Secretary had come in again quietly. "We're agreed that this nettle will have to be grasped and that to do so ourselves would raise very grave difficulties. On the other hand there's an outside chance that somebody else may do it for us."

"What chance?" the General asked. He sounded genuinely surprised.

They're not acting now, Mr. Secretary thought, not putting up a show for the Yankee. Something quite unexpected has happened.

The General said again, "What chance?"

"I didn't have time to tell you before but a little less than an hour ago I had an urgent call from a hotel in this city. It was the Greek Foreign Minister, alone except for a guard, and *incognito*. He said it was very urgent."

"It must be."

"Have I your permission to hear him?"

The General considered, said finally: "Yes. I know you won't get twisted by a Greek."

"That's kind of you, sir."

"You have my confidence." The General rose and bowed to Elliot Lash. "Then if it suits you, Mr. Secretary, perhaps this meeting had better stand adjourned."

The two Ministers were sitting across a table. The atmosphere wasn't actively hostile but both men were as wary as new girls in a cathouse. The Greek said stiffly:

"It is kind to see me at such short notice."

"A pleasure."

"For once we have a real interest in common."

"If you mean the South of that island I quite agree."

"I have come to make you a proposition. But first there is a condition precedent."

"That doesn't sound encouraging."

"I don't think you'll find it difficult to concede. Anything we decide between us is between our two countries and nobody else. It doesn't go near the United Nations."

The Turk laughed heartily, "No concession at all. Nobody wants the UN in his private affairs. They're impotent but would try to get in on the act. If they did they'd almost certainly wreck it."

"Thank you," the Greek said. "Then to business." He put his hands on the table, palms down, and drew a breath. His nails were not entirely clean. "We've got to get rid of Hezbollah from the South. If we don't it will become a new base for them. *You* can't do it without an international outrage. *We* just might. *With your agreement*."

"Go on."

"We have troops there but they're not decisively armed. The terms of the Ceasefire – "

"I know them too."

"A firefight with a hundred well-armed men is bound to result in heavy casualties. We need heavy armour and we're not allowed it. We therefore need a blind eye from you."

"But I thought – "

"I know. The accepted wisdom is that armour is useless in built-up areas. The Israelis found that out in Beirut. But the circumstances here are exceptional. No doubt you know the position as well as I do. Hezbollah occupies four houses on one side of a square, but in the middle of the square is an open garden. Put tanks with heavy guns in that garden and you could shell the houses to rubble at leisure. At the back of them is another street but that could be made a killing ground by interlocking fire from machine guns."

"You seem to have it all worked out."

"It was the military who made the plan."

"Then one thing occurs to me. You have some ordinary field artillery. Why not use that?"

The Greek said patiently: "Because we do not dare. To deploy unarmoured artillery within range of men with automatic weapons is something no professional soldier will do."

The Turk thought it over; he was quietly impressed; finally he asked deliberately: "What sort of tanks do you want and how many?"

"Tanks with a hundred-and-twenty millimetre guns. Four of them to do the job properly. Of course we should withdraw them once it was done."

. . . Like hell you would but that's a problem for later.

"Four tanks sounds rather a lot. Say two."

"Very well." The Greek was secretly pleased but concealed it. Two were what the soldiers had asked for.

"And what do we get out of this?" It was the Turk.

"The destruction of a hundred men who in time will threaten you as much as us."

"We might want something more than that. Some immediate and tangible quid pro quo."

The Greek said softly: "I believe that your Province is short of police. If we discovered that they'd been reinforced from the mainland it would be our turn to look the other way."

"Two hundred more police?"

"I can go to a hundred."

"Military police?"

"No, certainly not. That would be to increase your military strength."

"Agreed."

It was the Turk's turn to feel satisfaction. These men would not be regular soldiers but the Greek had made a concession unwittingly. Gendarmerie weren't technically soldiers but a hundred armed men would be a very real bonus. "And there's one other thing."

"I have offered my quid pro quo."

"This isn't another demand in any way but a matter to

155

our mutual interest. We shall need to know when your attack begins." The Greek looked surprised but the Turk went on. "Gunfire in your capital will be heard over most of the northern Province. It will cause civilian alarm which we cannot prevent but if the noise of battle arrives without warning there are people who might do more than just take fright. You follow me?"

"I follow you perfectly. I will see that you are told when a time has been arranged."

"Thank you. We are agreed, then?"

"Entirely." The two men shook hands, not with warmth but in amity. Both were thinking the same though neither said it. For both it had been an excellent bargain.

*   *   *

Daoud was talking again to his Chief of Staff. "The news is very bad indeed. A German called von Ems has taken a hand. He's an industrialist with a large interest in mining and he's flying down to talk to Ali Khan."

"That's ominous."

"You understate it. If control of that mine should pass to von Ems our plan to acquire it ourselves would collapse. We have sympathisers in Germany, plenty, including a man in his private office from whom I received the news of this flight. But we don't have any active cells. Perhaps we could contrive his murder, even with GSG 9 now on top, but his premature death is the last thing we want. What we want is financial control of that mine, which means taking its owner alive and holding him. We can't do that in Germany so control must stay here with the Maharajah till we're ready to persuade him to give it up."

The Chief of Staff said: "A tallish order."

"But for our friend in von Ems's office I dare say it would be quite impossible." Daoud spread a map of Europe and pointed. "He starts from his silly Bavarian castle or rather from an airfield near it. That brings him across south-eastern Europe, then he lands at the

Province's only airport." Daoud changed the map to one of the island. "At five points this brings him within range of the South. Where we have men."

"With machine guns and now three armoured cars. The chances of their hitting an aircraft – "

"I wasn't thinking of smallarms fire or even of the guns on those armoured cars. I was thinking of shoulder-fired SAMs."

"We don't have any."

"*They* don't have any. We do. We can't drop them on the square in the capital so they'll be dropped on the villa at midnight precisely. Five of them. There won't be time for proper practice nor the missiles to waste on it. You should arrange five separate parties, each with a launcher." Daoud marked five crosses on the map of the island. "These positions seem to give the best chance."

"And the ETA of the aircraft?"

Daoud told him.

The aircraft was called an executive jet, a description which Baron von Ems thought pretentious. At the moment it was carrying seven, two pilots and a stewardess, von Ems himself and his mistress of the moment who spoke with a North German accent which at times drove von Ems to something near frenzy, a legal adviser and the mandatory bodyguard without whom he never moved outside his fortified house.

He was quietly confident of success. He had approached Sir Henry Lash who had been discreet, but he knew that Sir Henry had been down to the island and he would hardly have troubled to make such a journey unless he had seen at least a case for the Maharajah to sell his holding.

And he had private reasons for wanting it badly. His father had been a fanatical Nazi, not sufficiently prominent to have been put before a Tribunal for War Crimes, but well enough known to have attracted attention. There was an Organisation with a capital letter

157

which was known to maintain a private Black List and the Baron's father had known he was on it. And one day he had been found drowned in his lake. There hadn't been a mark on his body, his heart was sound and he was an excellent swimmer.

His son was not a neo-Nazi, indeed he genuinely thought Hitler wicked. But in company which he felt he could trust he would admit after a drink or two that not all his ideas had been equally unsound. The pyrites and what it contained went to Israel.

It wouldn't if the Baron controlled the mine.

It was twelve o'clock and he summoned the stewardess, telling her to bring champagne. She was returning with a laden tray when she dropped it with a crash and fell down. There'd been an explosion outside the plane which had rocked it. When it had settled von Ems went forward. The pilot flying the aircraft was white and tense. The other was talking into his radio fast.

"What in hell was that?"

The pilot didn't answer him.

There was a small hinged seat and von Ems sat down in it. They flew on for maybe twenty seconds. Another loud bang and this time von Ems saw the flash through the window. The plane rocked again but the pilot corrected it. Then he said grimly:

"We're under fire."

The von Ems had been soldiers before they'd become tycoons. The Baron asked coolly: "What to do?"

"I'm going to pull away to the north. I'm going to climb as high as she'll go."

It was an irony to make the old gods laugh for the change of course gave the third missile a target. They were heat-seekers but not the latest and they couldn't lock on over very short distances before their own impetus carried them out of range. A minimal skill with the launcher was vital, and this the Hezbollah men had not been taught. But the handful of seconds as the jet changed course and climbed had given the

158

third missile a chance to lock on. Once it had done so the aircraft was dead.

The next explosion was enormously louder. Von Ems was thrown off his seat but could still see. What was left of the starboard wing was blazing, the pilot was fighting his stick but hopelessly. There was another and even louder bang as the fuel tank on the wing exploded. The plane went down in a flaming spiral, breaking up in the air as it fell to its death.

The debris fell on both sides of the border.

*   *   *

The meeting had been reconvened but events had overtaken it and it had had nothing to do but accept the arrangements made. Which with luck would destroy Hezbollah in the South. News that a German industrialist's aircraft had been shot down whilst in passage across the island had reached them just before they broke up but only Elliot Lash and the General had the knowledge to make a good guess at the motive and that knowledge was not for sharing generally. So it was probably an act of pure terror, one more reason for destroying Hezbollah.

Which was what they had come to Ankara to achieve.

So three men flew out of Ankara that evening. Two of them were quietly satisfied and only Mehmet Eldem was ill at ease.

The Greek was happy that he had brought back a success, and one at a price below his ceiling. For the Turk hadn't pressed him as hard as he might have, perhaps because he too was scared. The Greek had gone to Ankara with his Cabinet's knowledge but not with its universal approval, and one of the most powerful dissenters was also his personal rival in politics. Now his colleagues would applaud him thankfully and he'd be one rung advanced on his private ladder.

Elliot Lash was also pleased. He had expected to be asked to concede something, probably money or maybe arms; or he might have to show his country's displeasure and if necessary to hint at its power. Instead they had found their own solution. And he'd be home for his weekly game of tennis. Just tennis without qualification. The other game was called lawn tennis. He was no longer the first class player he had been but was still formidable on the hazard side. Anything loose he would put away firmly. His weekly not-too-serious game was as much a part of his well-ordered life as his comfortable home and a job he enjoyed. Or enjoyed when the President wasn't on his back.

Well, the President would accept this one happily. It didn't involve the United States; it was the sort of wheeler-dealing he understood; and it didn't risk a row inside NATO. Moreover the decision had already been taken and Mr. President was in no mood to make them himself. Especially minor ones about faraway countries whose position on the map he barely knew. For he was up to his eyes in something much bigger and would sell his unsatisfied soul to bring it off. He wished to go down in his country's history as something more than its favourite grandfather. To this end he was making enormous concessions to a Power which up to now he had reviled. Interests previously regarded as sacrosanct were being traded as though they were blocks of votes.

Especially the President's allies' interests.

So only Mehmet Eldem was less than content. When he had been despatched to Ankara he had expected to be coolly received, very possibly more severely than that. That hadn't happened: on the contrary he'd been treated with a calculated respect, and at a final *tête-à-tête* before he'd left, the General had been frank as never before . . . The arrangements made to defeat Hezbollah were promising, but in no way decisive until completed. Which could hardly be for ten days at least. Allow eight days to bring those tanks over and two more to plan the attack in detail. And for those ten

160

days the Province was still wide open, this time not to Greek mercenary amateurs but to Hezbollah in all its dedicated ruthlessness.

Mehmet Eldem had risen to take his leave but the General had had more to say. He'd had a signal from the Brigadier who would give Mehmet Eldem the details when he returned. Meanwhile its gist was at best alarming. Intelligence from the South was now excellent and it suggested that Hezbollah now had light armour. Armoured cars with four- or six-pounders – two or maybe three of them. No, they hadn't come in completely assembled – that was something which even Hezbollah couldn't contrive – but major units had been landed by night, engine, chassis, gun and tracks, and in one case they'd been landed by force. Coastguards had been killed in an affray. Colonel Eldem wouldn't welcome this news and the General welcomed it even less. The police reinforcements could be used to seal the coast but armoured cars could make mincemeat of the dividing fence.

And then the General had thrown his grenade almost casually. "When I appointed you you were discreetly incurious. I remember telling you that guessing wasn't a court martial offence. And no doubt you did. I mean about the mine."

"It wasn't difficult – other people did too. For instance those PLO who attacked it. And no doubt these new Hezbollah men have guessed too. But even with two or three armoured cars I don't think they've much chance of destroying it."

"They don't mean to destroy it. They mean to capture it."

"That would be even harder."

"No." The General had drawn in a very long breath. "Since you're going back to God knows what it's only proper you should know the whole story. You know that a British company owns the mine." The General let the breath out slowly. *"You don't know that the company is controlled by the Maharajah outright."*

161

Mehmet Eldem was silent, thinking hard. The implications had made his hands sweat unpleasantly. "Who else knows this besides you and now me?"

"The Man. The Maharajah himself and his financial adviser."

"Does Hezbollah know?"

"I can't say they don't. They have very good Intelligence, sympathisers in every country in Europe. Or they could be seeing it as a working hypothesis, one which might fit the few known facts."

What Mehmet felt first was a sharp irritation. "But this has stood the situation on its head. To those Greeks His Highness was a prime target for murder: Hezbollah will want him alive to play with." He added sourly as he felt was justified: "We can certainly use those police reinforcements."

"Who won't be with you for several days, nor the tanks to put an end to Hezbollah."

Mehmet's annoyance returned more strongly. "You're sending me into battle unarmed, sir."

"You knew that from the first."

"This is different. I realise you can't help me materially but you owe me a concession."

"State it."

"There are two people on the island who are much cleverer than I am. I'd like your permission to take their advice and that means telling the whole of the story."

"Tell me who they are," the General said.

"One is Miss Withers whose mother you once knew well." Mehmet was past any care for the niceties.

If this was an impertinence the General didn't seem to notice it. "Miss Withers will be entirely secure. If you wish to seek her advice you may do so. And the other man or woman?"

"James Wedder. He – "

"I have heard of James Wedder and I liked what I was told. He stood up for us once when we needed friends badly. If you wish to consult him too you may."

"And the Maharajah?"

"He is entitled to know the extent of his danger. But no more than that. And now if that is all – "

The General rose.

Mehmet Eldem was driven from the airport to his flat. He needed to sleep but knew that he wouldn't. His powers had not been increased: his liabilities had. The General had said that the Province was wide open. It was alarmingly clear that so too was he.

PART FOUR

The Pawns

Helen's villa was the most centrally placed and Mehmet and James Wedder had gone there, one to talk and the other to listen. Helen and James Wedder had sat in silence but with a visibly increasing alarm. When Mehmet had told his story James Wedder said:

"So until those tanks have destroyed Hezbollah the Maharajah is out on a very long limb. Naturally you have warned him."

"Of course. Most of the gendarmerie – our gain from the bargain struck with Greece – have been used to seal the northern coast but one or two are left over from that and I was able to offer increased protection. He turned it down flat."

"He would," Helen said, "he's as stubborn as I am." She gave Mehmet Eldem a small smile of apology. "People like us can make life difficult – I mean for those who are trying to help. But being watched and restricted, the knowledge that you're officially guarded – well, it doesn't suit our temperaments at all."

"So I have observed," Mehmet said. It was amicable but faintly acid.

James Wedder knew that both had tempers and he intervened smoothly to douse any danger. "We can leave that for the moment," he said. "Tell us what happened when you called on His Highness."

Mehmet Eldem did so dourly. He had been received with an impenetrable courtesy . . . Since the General had seen fit to disclose it, it was a fact that he, the Maharajah, owned almost all the equity of the company which leased the mine from the Province; and yes, the Baron von Ems, who had huge interests in mining, had been arriving to discuss a possible sale. He had been brutally prevented from doing so and there was only one possible motive for that, which was to ensure that control of the mine should stay with himself. He wasn't, if he might say so, quite stupid, and he'd realised the implications of that.

Then would he agree to leave the island? For a matter of ten days or so.

Certainly not. He wasn't going to be run out of his home by people he himself despised and whom his ancestors had employed as slaves.

Then Mehmet could offer increased protection.

Again unnecessary. He had sent for replacements for the two guards he had lost. He had been too courteous to mention Mrs. Meysey du Pres but the thought had been between them, almost tangible . . . If you couldn't protect my unfortunate mistress what value would be your protection to myself?

So good morning, Colonel Mehmet Eldem. And thank you.

The majordomo had shown Mehmet out.

James Wedder asked flatly: "So what do you do?"

"I can do nothing but the Brigadier can and has. The Maharajah was not cooperative but the Brigadier has been pulling the stops out. I would guess that the General has had a quiet word with him." Mehmet did what Daoud had done and spread a map, but this time it was one of the Province. "This is the Maharajah's house and this is the wire which runs up to the mountains. Just inside it is a road which is regularly patrolled but between that road and the house is open grassland. I'd have used a small part of the new gendarmerie to defend that strip of grass. By weapon pits and maybe a minefield. The same on the flanks. That house would have been a minor fortress against what now must be an attack by land. And, as I told you, they now have armoured cars."

"Then why don't you do it and damn His Highness's pride?"

"Because that land belongs to him. If I fortified it without his permission he would take it as a personal insult. He'd go straight to the Man and raise much trouble . . ."

"He'd do that all right," Helen Withers said. "I know him well enough to know that."

Mehmet gave her a glance but her face told him nothing. "So we're back to that road and the patrols which use it. Up to now they've been fairly casual affairs – an armed jeep and a single lorry of infantry. Now they've been stepped up considerably. The command jeep and the infantry are still there but between them goes a fast light tank. It's obsolete but can keep up with wheeled vehicles and it carries a gun which can mince any armoured car. And the frequency of the patrols has been stepped up too. They used to be hourly but now they're every twenty minutes."

James Wedder had been working it out. "So at any given point in the wire there's twenty minutes between patrols?"

"No. The patrols come back as well as go out and a returning patrol starts ten minutes after one has arrived. That cuts the uncovered time to ten minutes."

"Will Hezbollah know this?"

"There's no reason why they shouldn't. They can watch the patrols from the other side of the wire."

"So they'll know they have at the most ten minutes. That means choosing the shortest route to the target." Wedder put a finger on the map. "That's here – bang opposite the Maharajah's house. Why not put a standing patrol there?"

"We thought of that but the Brigadier turned it down. It's a balance of disadvantages, you see. If they see there's a static defence at one point, they will probably try somewhere else, further off. That would make it a longer run to the house and cut their time but with wheels under them they might make it up. Whereas if we're fairly sure of the point of attack the patrols will be specially vigilant near it. The Brigadier chose the latter and that was that. And as a good soldier he doesn't like fixed positions."

"But what about the fence?" Helen asked. "I thought it was electrified."

"It is. It's electrified against casual intruders but it's no obstacle to men taught to deal with it. They could short-circuit it or blow it with a shell. Either would raise an alarm in headquarters and also show the point of attack. Headquarters would radio to the two nearest patrols. Which would naturally put on all possible speed. Thereby cutting the time again. We hope."

There was a silence before James Wedder spoke again. "If I were a bookmaker I'd give forty to one against success. But I can't help admiring them."

"So do I in my way. The motives which drive them have never touched me and their methods I find entirely repulsive. But unquestionably they're very brave men. Send them on a suicide mission and they feel proud."

James Wedder would have lost his bet, for the attackers were the cream of Hezbollah, men ready to die, even eager to do so. Which had given to Daoud, who'd slipped into the island, an option which regular soldiers had not foreseen. He had ordered two diversionary attacks, one on each side of the point of attack, which in fact had been where Wedder had foreseen. Daoud had three armoured cars and he sacrificed two of them. Each of them was to engage a passing patrol. They'd be unsupported by infantry, which was needed for the main attack, and in any case were hopelessly outgunned by a tank. These were suicide missions and the car-crews had known it but they had gone without demur, even smiling.

The tanks had duly smashed them to matchwood but the engagements had taken several minutes and minutes were more important to Daoud than lives.

He was leading the main assault in person for he would have considered it a disgrace not to do so. You didn't send men on a mission you shirked yourself. The electrified fence had been professionally neutralised and the third armoured car went through it like butter. The men on foot came behind it and went in.

They had practised the assault more than once and they did it with panache and style. On this open grassland there was almost no cover but one section advanced whilst another, lying behind it, gave covering fire. Then it leapfrogged through the first in attack. It was classical infantry tactics but costly. The guards had no prepared positions and were shooting from the mansion's windows, but all of them had once been soldiers and all of them were competent riflemen. Hezbollah men began to drop and for a moment the forward movement wavered. Then the armoured car came up behind them. Shooting from windows the guards had no chance against shells. When all had been silenced Hezbollah took the house. His Highness was unarmed and they took him too. They left behind them eleven dead men.

Later, when Turkish soldiers arrived, they began to collect the bodies methodically. But one of them was not yet dead. He was lying on his face, quite motionless, but he was holding a grenade to his stomach. When two soldiers bent over him he pulled the pin.

*   *   *

Mehmet Eldem was feeling frustrated and angry for he couldn't make Helen and James Wedder understand. He had excellent English – he even thought in it – and a formidable vocabulary; but he couldn't contrive to take them with him. You couldn't say 'private honour' to the English. They'd be far too polite to laugh but they'd surely blush.

And both of them had been intolerably reasonable, which made it worse. An honourable defeat, they had pointed out, was not a matter for feeling shame, and if anyone should fall on his sword it was the Brigadier, not

Mehmet Eldem. For the Brigadier had been humiliatingly outguessed. And on top of that Mehmet had been in an impossible position; the General had sold him an impossible task and almost nothing with which to carry it out. What he was now proposing was nonsense.

None of this had soothed his mental wound. The General had called the job anomalous which Mehmet had thought an understatement but in a way it could be simply defined: it had been to keep the island out of the news, to minimise Greek malice from the South, to let the salve of time do its healing work. No scandals, above all things no headlines. He had realised that he would need great good luck but he hadn't been ready to face retirement. He had accepted the job and done so gratefully.

All this he had explained to his friends and both had been generously sympathetic. But he could see that he hadn't touched their minds as his own was clouded with bitter shame. Helen was saying in that reasonable way of hers:

"I follow all that – you've had rotten luck. But it wasn't your fault that Hezbollah set up in the South. That made it quite a different job."

"I dare say it did but I didn't resign."

"I think you're being a trifle White Knightish."

"I don't. If we don't recover the Maharajah there could be war. At the best there'll be worldwide, enormous headlines, which is precisely what I was appointed to prevent."

Helen asked anxiously: "Will they be torturing him?"

"Not yet if they're at all up to date, which the way they handled the actual attack suggests they are. Put a man on the rack or its modern equivalent and he'll say anything to get himself off it. That statement you have to check for the truth. Even the Inquisition knew that and it usually tried persuasion first. Modern persuasion means narco-interrogation. It's unpleasant but it doesn't cause physical pain. But that could come later. I've got to go."

172

"But going off alone like that – "

"But what else can I do but go alone? If I'm captured or killed there'll be awkward questions but I shan't be a Turkish soldier in uniform. If I took such men with me that would be a straightforward invasion and the Greeks would squeeze the last drop from the orange. Besides, the Brigadier wouldn't stand for it; he wouldn't give me a single man. But he sees the affair in the same light as I do and he's prepared to give me arms and transport."

"Then let's have it again," James Wedder said. "The whole crazy plan."

"The one thing I have in my favour is time, for they've told us when the tanks are going to attack." Mehmet looked at his watch. "It is now seven o'clock on Tuesday evening and the attack goes in at midnight tomorrow. That's twenty-nine hours to get to the villa. Plenty. I've got to assume that they're holding him there but it's where they held their previous hostages."

"A fair enough assumption. Go on."

"I don't dare fly over Greek-held territory and in any case I haven't been taught to drop. So I shall drive to our other port on the panhandle which will cut the distance by sea by half. Courtesy of the Brigadier I shall there find a suitable boat with a motor and there'll be plenty of time to reach the villa by midnight." Mehmet opened a briefcase and laid out photographs. "These were taken some time ago but I've no reason to think that the layout has changed much. As you see, that villa is a considerable establishment. It once belonged to a Frenchman. Odd, that. The French hardly ever take holidays outside France. But there it is, complete with private beach and landing stage. If that's patrolled I shall have to swim for it. And I'll have to tow my arms in a waterproof bag."

"And what can you possibly do with those arms?"

"I see it like this. Please correct me if you see a fallacy. The shelling will start at midnight precisely and at a distance of ten miles or less will be audible in that villa clearly. To the men who are holding His Highness

173

in it the most likely reason for heavy gunfire is that their main body is being attacked in the capital."

"Agreed. And so?"

"So their first thought will be to try and join them. They'll guess there'll be a roadblock between them so they'll take the Maharajah as hostage. But if they think they're being attacked themselves they'll probably stay and fight it out."

"Attacked by a single man?"

"They won't know that. I shall take an assault rifle and as many RP grenades as I can tote. Moving about in the dark from place to place you'd be astonished what a diversion one man can create."

"Very well, I'm astonished. But how does this help the Maharajah?"

"It doesn't as a matter of course but as I see it there's an outside chance. Look at it from the point of view of desperate men. Your main body is being attacked in its citadel and something is going on outside which could well be a probe before a formal attack. You don't think of your prisoner first: you rush to arms."

"Leaving your hostage unguarded?"

"It's possible. If you're only a handful of men in the villa and the racket outside sounds convincing enough. No better than that but it's all I have."

Wedder thought this over for nearly a minute; at last he said with a deliberate casualness: "Two men would double the noise. I'm coming too."

There was a shaken silence before Helen broke it. "But what could you do?" It was tactless to the verge of brutality but Helen had been surprised into both.

Wedder showed no offence but answered coolly. "I could double the fire-power. I've never fired a grenade in my life but I was once in a rather dangerous posting and they taught us how to use an LMG. Very undiplomatic but there it was." He added on a faint note of pride: "I can even clear a simple stoppage."

Mehmet Eldem said firmly: "It's out of the question."

James Wedder went on as though not hearing him,

174

as though only the details remained to be discussed. "An LMG has a lot more fire-power than the assault rifle Mehmet was thinking of taking, and if he doesn't have to carry that he can carry more grenades with the launcher."

"I repeat that it's quite out of the question. I simply refuse to take you with me."

James Wedder began to laugh but checked it. "You can't do that and I'll tell you why. I'd go straight to the Man and spill the whole story. The Brigadier is one thing, the Man another. In another age and another country the Brigadier would be ritually disembowelling himself so he'll cooperate with you up to a point. The Man will not. He'll see this whole thing as the adventure it is and if you insist he'll have you arrested. By the police."

"But that would be blackmail." Mehmet Eldem was shocked.

"Of course it would. But you forget that I was once a diplomat and ninety per cent of all diplomacy is just that. If you want it in rather grander words ninety per cent of all diplomacy is the calculated application of power short of war. I have the power to inhibit your plan."

"Obtained unfairly. I thought I could trust you."

"And I thought you had once been a Military Attaché. Did you learn nothing of how things really work? I'm coming with you or you're simply not going."

Mehmet realised he'd have to switch lines and did so. "You realise that it's exceptionally dangerous?"

"And you, my friend, know something about me which I don't want to have to put into words."

Mehmet needed none to understand. This man's life could be measured in months, perhaps days. Better a violent end in combat than lying in a hospital bed, dying slowly of increasing doses of a drug. He nodded approvingly; he'd have felt the same.

"You have me where it hurts. Very well."

Helen rose and left the room silently. She wasn't a

175

woman to use tears as a weapon and she didn't wish men to see her weeping.

When she had gone James Wedder said softly: "You know what she's thinking?"

"No, I can't read her or not all the time."

"I've known her longer than you and I sometimes can. She's facing the embarrassing thought that if only one of us comes back from this it would be convenient if that one were you."

Mehmet still had reasonable doubts about James Wedder's skill with a light machine gun but none about his competence at sea. He had known that he kept a sailing boat but not that when *en poste* here earlier he had kept a fair-sized cabin cruiser in one of the little ports on the southern coast. James Wedder knew these waters well and they weren't at all as innocuous as they looked. Mehmet knew nothing of navigation beyond that he could read a compass and with this and the lights from the buildings ashore – he had intended to hug the coast as close as he dared.

James Wedder had laughed at this: it hadn't been on. There were shoals and in some places hidden reefs. Mehmet would have holed the boat or at best got her helplessly stuck on a sandbank. You had to go out quite a way to be safe. There were charts in a locker but Wedder didn't refer to them. He knew what he was doing perfectly, moving about the boat efficiently, sometimes singing, as gay as a bridesmaid.

Mehmet frowned, a soldier's instincts uneasy. He had seen this before and he thought it ominous. Men who went into battle glum and tense – sometimes they came back in one piece; but men who went in cavalierly offended the gods and invited disaster. As often as not, he'd observed, *hubris* was punished.

Presently Wedder looked at his watch. "I think you said to arrive at twenty-three thirty. We've made very good time and don't want to be early. I think we could stop and eat our rations."

"On this boat," Mehmet said, "you're the evident master."

They opened a wickerwork hamper and ate. There was cold chicken and salad, fruit and a bottle of wine. Helen had chosen their last supper handsomely. Over the meal Wedder chatted easily, and again Mehmet Eldem, who'd seen serious fighting, was anxious for a man who had not. He might have been on some casual picnic and now was saying equally casually:

"There's something all wrong with this plan, you know."

"If you mean we've only a hope in a hundred – "

"I didn't mean that. I meant Hezbollah."

"What about Hezbollah?"

"They're mad."

It occurred to Mehmet to say: "So are we," but he preferred to listen to Wedder carefully. Instinct told him that Wedder was going to die; and experience that with death's hand on their shoulder men sometimes had an uncanny prevision. "Go on," he said.

"It's hard to put into sensible words something which has just occurred to you. But suppose Hezbollah doesn't stay and fight."

"You mean if they run for the capital and their friends?"

"No, I don't think they'll do that if we make enough noise. Let me think." Mehmet let him. Finally Wedder said uncertainly: "If they think we're thirty or forty men they may do something we haven't thought of. They're not like the PLO at all. The PLO who attacked the mine were brave men who were prepared to die. But they hoped that they wouldn't; they weren't looking for a martyr's crown. Hezbollah is – they're dedicated and therefore abnormal. They might not choose to fight it out in the villa, they might prefer to die sensationally."

"Such as how?"

"If they think we're two platoons at least they might choose to come out and take us on. They might think that better than dying singly in room-to-room fighting they're bound to lose."

177

Mehmet Eldem was uneasily silent for the PLO had done just that at the mine. They'd been caught in the open, then charged men in weapon pits. And the PLO had been normal men, not dedicated religious fanatics. He thought carefully before he spoke again.

"You talked of something we hadn't thought of. A desperate charge is one of them. Anything else?"

James Wedder said surprisingly: "No. Half a minute ago I was seeing quite clearly. Now whatever it was has totally gone." His voice had gone back to the matter-of-fact and he looked at his watch again. "It's time to move on."

They approached the little jetty cautiously for if it was patrolled they'd have to fight, and a preliminary skirmish was the last thing Mehmet Eldem wanted. But it wasn't and they crept ashore, dropping behind the first cover they saw, inspecting the scene which lay before them by the light of what was left of a fading moon. Mehmet realised that so far luck had been with them, for the slope which led up to the ugly villa was covered by scrub and occasional rocks. A single paved path joined the boathouse to the villa itself but to either side the ground had not been cleared. It was very much better country for infantry than the open grassland round His Highness's house where Hezbollah had lost eleven men. In the villa only one room was lighted.

. . . That's where they're keeping the Maharajah. Perhaps he's being deprived of sleep or maybe he's already sedated.

As they watched, a sentry appeared from behind the house. He walked along the terrace which framed it, then turned left and went behind again. A minute later he reappeared. Circular tour, Mehmet thought; he whispered to Wedder:

"Go to your first position left of the path. Wait till that man comes round again, then take him. Move to another position at once, then fire at the windows. Any window but that lighted one. When I hear you open I'll open myself."

James Wedder nodded and moved away. Mehmet noticed that he didn't shake hands.

But of course he hadn't. That would seem theatrical, anathema to a good New Englander.

He moved to his own first position and waited. Presently the sentry came back from behind the house. There was a single brief burst of fire and he fell.

. . . He wasn't boasting when he said he could shoot.

Simultaneously Mehmet heard distant gunfire. Instantly every window was lighted. Heads appeared silhouetted against them, firing automatic weapons into the darkness beyond the pool of the villa's lights. Mehmet Eldem shook his head disapprovingly. The trouble with giving men automatics too early was that you skimped on the basic lessons of marksmanship. These men should be looking for targets and picking them off, not blindly browning at where a target might be. The practice degraded an infantryman's craft but nowadays seemed to be universal. The Americans had done the same in Vietnam, driving out on roads in armoured vehicles, never leaving them to patrol on foot but blazing into the cover each side of them. They had called it a prophylactic shoot and another country called it reconnaissance by fire. Whatever you called it, it was very poor soldiering, no substitute for the discipline of a patrol. Mehmet snorted.

Unlike the man who had brought down the Baron Mehmet understood his weapon. He sighted carefully at the nearest window and fired. The grenade went cleanly through it and burst. The light went out and the firing from that room stopped dead.

In the second of silence which followed Mehmet listened. Away to his right he could hear the tanks' guns. They seemed to be firing in salvoes now, and after each came the angry chatter of small arms. Men would be running from crumbling buildings. Those who ran forward would be cut down by the tanks and those who attempted escape at the back would run into a murderous crossfire.

. . . Poor brave, committed, suicidal fools.

And the men in this villa were in no way different. Mehmet wondered what they'd do next: he couldn't guess. Wedder had suggested they might charge with the bayonet but Mehmet considered that improbable. Behind walls they had cover but in the open, against the lighted house, they'd have none.

What they did for the moment was to fire more furiously. A burst fell within a yard of Mehmet and he decided it was time to move. He crawled to another position and sighted again. To his left he could hear James Wedder's LMG. He seemed to be shooting more than competently. A window opposite him was lighted still but no heads were visible and no fire came from it.

Mehmet nuzzled the launcher, took final aim. Suddenly there was silence again. A total and astonished silence.

A man in pyjamas had come out onto the lighted terrace. He was unsteady on his feet and fell. For a moment he lay still, then struggled upright. He staggered to the balustrade and held on.

. . . So when the firing started his guard did leave him. He didn't bother to tie him up since evidently he's doped to the eyes. If he weren't he'd have made for the back of the house.

The Maharajah felt his way by the stonework, working towards the path which divided it. When he reached it he stood up straight but swayed. Without the balustrade for support he was almost helpless. A single shot came from the villa and missed.

Or had it missed? There was another shot but His Highness kept moving.

They're teasing him, Mehmet thought. They're animals. They'll let him get to the bottom and then kill.

Another man had come out of the scrub on the left and instantly automatic fire raked him. But he was running fast, bent almost double, jinking like a snipe, a poor target for men who were poorer marksmen. He

180

reached the path and the staggering Maharajah, trying to pull him the few feet into cover. Both for a moment were a stationary target and a hail of fire cut them mercilessly down.

"The fool," Mehmet said but he said it respectfully. He was wondering what he'd have done himself if he'd known that he was walking dead. Interesting but in no way fruitful. The play was over but not the epilogue. He would take as many with him as he could.

He took out another room with a grenade and was loading again when the villa collapsed. It fell inwards on itself and Hezbollah. Mehmet saw it first, then heard the explosions. Finally there was the blast of air. If he'd been standing it would have knocked him down.

The lights of the villa had gone out with its fall but Mehmet had a torch and used it. He ran to the path and the two men lying there. James Wedder had fallen on top of His Highness. His head was a bloody pulp. Mehmet rolled him off the Maharajah. The Maharajah was alive and just conscious. Most of his left leg had been shot away.

Mehmet Eldem hesitated. It went against every inherited instinct to leave his dead in the face of an enemy but this was an exceptional case. For one thing there was no enemy visible: no man in that villa could conceivably have survived; and for another the noise of the explosions which had destroyed it, separate charges but fired simultaneously, would certainly have been heard in the capital. Soon there would be soldiers or police and Wedder was an American citizen. America had a mission here which would see that he was decently buried.

Mehmet bent his strong shoulders and picked up His Highness. He groaned faintly but he didn't utter. He came of fighting stock and was proud.

Mehmet carried him down the path to the jetty. Getting him into the boat was difficult, for the Maharajah couldn't help himself. He was just conscious and in evident pain but he didn't complain.

181

Mehmet went out to sea at least a mile, then turned sharply to port. Without James Wedder he was going to need much luck in getting home.

He prayed for it.

*   *   *

Mehmet Eldem had been called to Ankara and the General had received him warmly. Mehmet knew that he had good reason to do so for the tide on the island was running strongly their way. The ruthless crushing of Hezbollah's main body, even something of the affair at the villa – these were matters which couldn't be hushed up completely. But the publicity had on the whole been favourable. That part of the island still governed by Greeks had proved capable of defending itself. Just as Jordan had, and good luck to both of them. That had been the general line. The Arab press had of course been outraged, and in the United Nations the Arab chorus had sent up a louder than usual lament. But the United Nations was close to powerless and a recent procession of humiliating failures had eroded any authority it had had.

And there'd been another and clearly God-given benefit. So long as Hezbollah had had a base in the South it was a potential threat to the North as it grew in power, but before it had been finally crushed it had done the Province something more than a favour by eliminating the local Greek terrorists. For reasons of its own, no doubt, and not to oblige the Man in his Province. But no matter. Hezbollah had ruthlessly wiped them out and they wouldn't return.

Of course there were still little local difficulties. The South still had two battle tanks, the Province none, and it would be childish to suppose for a moment that the Greeks of the South would honour their promise to return these weapons to mainland Greece once their job was done. So the General would have to slip two battle tanks into the North. That was the way Near East

182

politics worked. He saw no reason whatever to feel ashamed.

The General sent for coffee and over it laughed. "And those aren't," he said, "the only things going for us. The Man is writing a new constitution and it's going to be ever-so democratic. Based on the Swiss, I hear – the Recall and all that. The sort of thing which was admired in the Thirties. There'll be universal suffrage of course, but God help you if you vote the wrong way. And when he gets out of hospital the Maharajah is going to be President. The whole thing will be an enormous sham – the Man will be boss as he always has been – but half-baked progressives will lap it up. I don't say there'll be an immediate rush to recognise the Province *de jure* – Greece and the United Nations will see to that – but at least it won't be quite the pariah it is. The Man is a very shrewd operator indeed."

Mehmet thought this over carefully. The implications were disagreeably clear. "Then you'll no longer need my humble services."

The General appeared surprised and was. "I don't know what makes you say that – it's nonsense. With luck I'll no longer need a trouble-shooter: what I shall need will be a formal representative. Diplomats being the me-toos they are other countries will be tempted to follow." The General looked at Mehmet urbanely. "Would you care for the job?"

"Do you think I could do it?"

"I don't see why not. You've never been fully debauched by diplomacy but as a Military Attaché you were near enough to realise it's a pretence. That gives you an enormous headstart." The General's voice became coolly ironic. "Ambassador and Plenipotentiary. Plenipotentiary means full of power, but the one thing you won't get from him is a decision on any matter on the spot. Instead he'll send a signal home. Nowadays he's a dressed-up office boy."

"You're offering me a job as an office boy?" It was Mehmet's turn to sound ironic.

"Not at all. The circumstances are quite exceptional. In practice you'll be my personal man and I expect you to behave as such. You will rank above the Brigadier."

"It sounds a bit of a burden."

"It is. But you've shown that you can carry it. That's settled then?"

Mehmet Eldem nodded.

"And I can think of other advantages too. Pay, for instance – a Major General's and an adequate *frais*. And security in one post for several years." The General's voice changed for the second time. "May we speak as friends?"

"I'd be greatly honoured."

"Then when I sent you to the Province first I ventured a remark about marriage and settling down. I hope you didn't think it impertinent."

This time Mehmet shook his head.

"In that case I will risk repeating it. An ambassador needs a wife rather badly."

"As it happens I need one badly too."

"You have formed an attachment?"

"I earnestly hope it will soon be more."

"Shall I be indiscreet if I ask – ?"

"The lady is Miss Helen Withers."

The General sprang to his feet and clapped like a Russian. "My very dear fellow! An admirable choice. Excellent blood on both sides of the family. Her father was clever, an eminent scientist, and her mother was a Dutchwoman who befriended us when we most needed friends. Sincerest congratulations."

"Thank you, but they're premature. Miss Withers still has wide interests in England. I doubt if she's really ready for marriage."

"Then make her ready."

"I'm afraid I don't follow."

"Come Colonel, you have proved you're not stupid. I have known only one European woman well and I dare say you have guessed who that was. But the relationship taught me one thing clearly. When it comes to a woman's unchanging instincts they're much the same the whole world over. A feminist would kill me for saying so, but nothing concentrates a woman's mind better than the knowledge she has a bun in the oven."

Mehmet stared at the General a little uncertainly, like a bright-eyed bird who'd been tempted by some unusual titbit. He could understand now why he'd risen to General and afterwards a great deal higher. Finally Mehmet said respectfully:

"Wouldn't that be rather outside the rules?"

"It depends how badly you want her in wedlock."

"Very badly indeed."

The General shrugged. "You're a diplomat now. The rules mean nothing."

Mr. Secretary of State Elliot Lash was well content. He mistrusted the word euphoria which he associated with some spiritual experience; and if he had felt such a thing or even its onset would have dealt with it by taking a purge. But he could permit himself to feel contented.

For, like the General, things had gone well for him. From his own and wider point of view a dangerous situation had come off the boil, and he began to count his blessings happily. First, an outlaw gang of religious fanatics could no longer do to that obscure little island what they'd already done to the state of Lebanon; their foothold, their base, their power to influence had been excised. To do so had needed cooperation, or collusion if you preferred to speak plainly, between Greeks and Turks. Who had been snapping at each other's heels for more centuries than Elliot Lash could remember. That they had reached a *combinazione* at all was something which certainly wouldn't last but the fact that they had temporarily done so took the pressure off a more serious problem.

Blessing Number Two, Lash reflected, for that divided island had been dangerous tinder to a war between two NATO allies. His country would have been caught

185

between the horns. Ostensibly it must stay strictly neutral, do its best to impose a ceasefire quickly, but when it came to the naked bones of *realpolitik* it couldn't afford to see Turkey defeated. Turkey was a valuable ally and Greece was not. In anything like a pinch she'd rat and meanwhile was a loud-mouthed nuisance.

He came to his third blessing and laughed, for this was something much more personal. Mr. President was off his back since he'd lost interest in the Near East and beyond it. He was playing for very high stakes indeed for he wanted a place in his country's history as something more than a two-term nonentity. Elliot Lash had warned him sharply – it was clearly his formal duty to do so. The President had taken this badly and now minimised contact with Mr. Secretary of State.

Which suited Mr. Secretary well. He had delivered his warning in very clear terms: it was no part of his duty to put political spokes in a President's wheel, certainly not to impose his own will on him. The President had been democratically elected (Hah!) and he had not. His conscience was clear and his days more peaceful.

And in his private life affairs went smoothly. One of his sons, the academic, had just been given a chair at Yale and could hope to be Master of one of its Colleges. Lash had three grandsons but had wanted a granddaughter and his daughter had just obliged him.

Finally there was tennis tomorrow. He was playing a man from his Department whom he disliked. The diplomat was the better player but inclined to be a trifle too classical. He had a beautiful stroke on his forehand, heavily cut, and could lay down a stream of formidable chases. But his backhand wasn't nearly so strong and he hated to be bustled about, particularly on the hazard side. So Elliot would bang the ball about, sophisticated beginner stuff, and if his tactics were right he was going to win. It wasn't permitted to play for money but this was a match on his club's private ladder and he knew where he could place a bet.

186

He had given himself an ample luncheon and now was feeling distinctly drowsy, but if someone came in and found him asleep the scandal would leak and spread alarmingly . . . Mr. Secretary Lash was over the top; he had even nodded off after lunch.

He decided he didn't care. He slept.

On the island Major Maurice Fazakerly was contented too. The English company which insured the Club had sent a man down to inspect the wreckage and he had hemmed and hawed on the terms of the small print. But one of Fazakerly's fellow expatriates had been a lawyer of experience and standing who had felt confident of his case and had argued it well. He'd been prepared to take it to court if need be, and the man from the insurance company had known that a precedent stood against him. Finally he had paid in full. A contract had been placed in Turkey (if it had gone to Greece the Man might have vetoed it) and the beginnings of a new Club were visible.

For Fazakerly and the others like him life could go on as it always had.

He was talking to his wife that evening, sitting in what she, a South African, still obstinately insisted on calling the stoep. She had heard it all before more than once but she let him drone on.

"Damned fine fellow, that Mehmet Eldem. Going off alone like that – "

"He didn't go alone. He took Wedder. Who didn't come back."

"A pity, that, but I dare say a blessing. I never met him but I knew his story. If I'd been in Wedder's shoes – "

"He's dead. His own people have looked after him. Stick to Colonel Eldem, please."

There was something in her manner he didn't like; she was going to say something quite insufferable. "I can only repeat – "

"You always do. But I've got something new."

"Then tell me."

187

"Your Mehmet Eldem is sparking Helen Withers."

"Is he indeed? He shows excellent taste."

Mrs. Fazakerly curled a thin upper lip. "He won't get her, of course."

"Whyever not?"

"In my country he'd be considered a Coloured."

He stared at her in a contempt he didn't hide. "Woman," he said, "you're a fool. You always were."

When Mehmet had returned from Ankara he had found a short letter from Helen Withers. It had worried him more than he cared to admit since she was going back to England on business. A fortnight at least, she had said, and he'd been counting the days. But here she was back after five, as at ease and as gay as he'd ever seen her. They were dining at Nico's again, and again she had ordered a gentle Beaujolais. She was saying, half as a tease and half seriously:

"I suppose I should call you Your Excellency now."

"That isn't public knowledge yet. Where did you get it?"

"The General wrote to me. In strictest confidence, of course. As a sincere and respectful friend of my mother – I quote him *verbatim* – he thought I was entitled to know."

"Why should he think that?"

"Work it out."

Mehmet Eldem wasn't overly pleased. The General might have been Helen's father, though Mehmet was perfectly sure he wasn't, but there was ground upon which even fathers trod warily. Helen might think it interference and that could easily turn against himself.

Apparently she had not for she was going on happily. "I went to England to tie up two loose ends. The Maharajah was first – he's still in a home there. In view of our relationship – there wasn't one but you know what I mean – I thought it would be at least polite to take His Highness a modest bunch of flowers." She added with

188

a suspicion of irony: "After all, he'd sent me flowers by the truckload."

"And how did you find him?"

"I didn't find him: his family had closed in like a curtain. His two sons were with him most of the day and even his wife had flown in from Nice. She had just left one of those drying-out places but she felt it her duty to be with her husband. The sons packed her back to Nice pretty quickly because they knew she could disgrace them in England. In a different way my presence might have done so too . . . Unknown woman turns up from the island . . . Those sons have become very English indeed." Helen shook her head emphatically. "There was no place for me in that sort of galley even if I had seriously wanted it. Which I had not."

"You did mention the subject once or twice."

"I'm a woman."

"So I gratefully observe. And the Maharajah himself?"

"I did get a word with a friendly matron. He has lost his left leg just above the knee and will need crutches for the rest of his life. But that won't stop him becoming President."

"That one isn't public either."

A little slyly she said: "I have very good sources."

"You have indeed."

"For an ambassador's wife they'll come in handy."

"An ambassador's *wife*?" He had spilt some wine saying it.

"Well, say an ambassador's recognised companion. That will do to start with, I think."

He was suspicious for this was going too easily. There was bound to be a snag. He asked carefully:

"And the other loose end you spoke of?"

"A job. You remember we talked about journalism once. You were sceptical and perfectly rightly."

"I'm sorry if I was tactless."

"Phooey! I can get all the tact I need from women. The second thing I want from a man is the certainty that he's telling me the truth." She added as an afterthought:

"And the knowledge that when I get too uppity he'll slap me down . . . Where was I?"

"Looking for work in Fleet Street."

"So I was. Work in women's journalism. And it took me just forty-eight hours to find out that I hadn't a hope in hell of getting it. There were various reasons, amongst them the closed shop you mentioned, but chiefly that they could still smell St. Mildred's. To the hard-working pro that's out, and out, and out."

"So what happens now?" Mehmet asked.

"I've had a bit of timely luck. Father went up to London a lot and in those days it was cheaper to keep a small flat. It's let at the moment but the lease runs out in a couple of months. I'd like to keep it on for myself if you don't object. I love this preposterous island of yours but if I stayed here all the year I'd go mad. Worse, I'd become a bore like the other old cats. You'd throw me out. So two or three times a year I'll go home and freshen up. That is, if you agree, of course."

He heard himself say quickly: "Agreed."

"Thank you, sir. And there are one or two things at this end too. For instance, I've fixed old Spiro, the boatman. I couldn't live here and feel beholden to him. He still doesn't know what really happened but I'd have drowned if he hadn't pulled me in. He wouldn't take naked money in any form but he's let me give him a new engine and a refit. I also gave him a steady retainer. When I'm here, which should be most of the year, he works for me and for nobody else. When I'm in England he can accept whatever trade there may be."

"Very generous," Mehmet Eldem said.

"And talking of money there's still that Picasso. The one you tried to fool me was stolen."

"That wasn't one of my better days." He hesitated but then asked it outright. "You are thinking of selling it?"

"No, not yet, but I've had an offer. From the same firm mother bought it from. A man came down and was very frank. In a few years time it may be worth a fortune but at the moment it is worth very little. There's

190

a risk and he was prepared to buy that risk. For a very substantial sum indeed."

"I'd rather you kept it, I'm not a rich man. We have land but I'm a younger son."

"You say you're not rich but you're very well off. You have an ambassador's salary and no doubt a pension. Capitalise that at, say, eight per cent and you'll find that you're a moneyed man."

He was silent and she was content he be so . . . If he sticks me with an enormous family I shan't make ooh-la-la about that. But a nice bit of capital would come in handy.

She had finished her coffee and shook her head at the offer of more. He paid the bill and they walked home arm in arm. From time to time he could feel her shiver but he knew that the shiver was not of fear. At the steps which led to the door they stopped.

"Come in for a nightcap," Helen said. She had contrived to keep her voice quite normal.

"There's nothing in the world I'd like more."

She stood aside to let him precede her. It was a gesture which he understood perfectly.

ρ